THE DUKE'S DESIRE

ERICA RIDLEY

The *12 Dukes of Christmas*:

Once Upon a Duke

Kiss of a Duke

Wish Upon a Duke

Never Say Duke

Dukes, Actually

The Duke's Bride

The Duke's Embrace

The Duke's Desire

Dawn With a Duke

One Night With a Duke

Ten Days With a Duke

Forever Your Duke

The *Dukes of War*:

The Viscount's Tempting Minx

The Earl's Defiant Wallflower

The Captain's Bluestocking Mistress

The Major's Faux Fiancée

The Brigadier's Runaway Bride

The Pirate's Tempting Stowaway

The Duke's Accidental Wife

Rogues to Riches:

Lord of Chance

Lord of Pleasure

Lord of Night

Lord of Temptation

Lord of Secrets

Lord of Vice

Gothic Love Stories:

Too Wicked to Kiss

Too Sinful to Deny

Too Tempting to Resist

Too Wanton to Wed

Magic & Mayhem:

Kissed by Magic

Must Love Magic

Smitten by Magic

The Wicked Dukes Club:

One Night for Seduction by Erica Ridley

One Night of Surrender by Darcy Burke

One Night of Passion by Erica Ridley

One Night of Scandal by Darcy Burke

One Night to Remember by Erica Ridley

One Night of Temptation by Darcy Burke

CRESSMOUTH GAZETTE

Welcome to Christmas!

Our picturesque village is nestled around Marlowe Castle, high atop the gorgeous mountain we call home. Cressmouth is best known for our year-round Yuletide cheer. Here, we're family.

The legend of our twelve dukes? Absolutely true! But perhaps not always in the way one might expect...

CHAPTER 1

November 1814
Marlowe Castle
Cressmouth, England

With her arms full of fresh-cut flowers nicked from the castle greenhouse, Meg Church burst into her best friend's gorgeous new office. Oh, very well, "Meg" had technically been christened Miss Margaret Damaris Brouillard-Church, but who wanted to waste time on anything that stuffy and boring?

This had been one of the *least* boring months in recent history. Meg's bosom friend Eve had fallen in love with one of the dashing le Duc brothers—the slightly less ridiculously handsome one, in Meg's studied opinion, although she wouldn't tell her bosom friend that. Eve had *married* Sébastien le Duc to the dismay of every unwed woman for miles, and now had her very own newspaper.

Marlowe Castle had purchased the Cressmouth Gazette from Eve's father, who'd wanted to shut it down when he retired. Instead, the castle solicitor had put long-suffering and hardworking Eve in charge. Wasn't that just the raisin in the pudding? Meg couldn't think of anyone more deserving.

"Here," she announced, as she began strategically arranging stems of yellow gorse. "If you're going to be cooped inside this enormous, luxurious new office all day and night, you need a bit of beauty to offset all those mountains of paper." She spun toward her friend with a mischievous shake of her finger. "Please tell me you're no longer spending your nights hunched over a printing press. I'm sure your husband can find a few other ways to entertain you."

Eve flushed scarlet and became extremely interested in inspecting her new desk's empty drawers.

"Marvelous!" Meg clapped her hands in

glee. "I had no doubt the le Duc brothers would be every bit as good as they look."

Eve sank back in her chair and covered her eyes.

"You can't get missish on me now—you're *married*," Meg teased her. "It's perfectly acceptable for you and your husband to perform as many decadent, carnal acts as can fit into a night. It's me who must be secretive about such things."

Eve peeked through her fingers, both eyebrows raised. "'Secretive?' You can't even be *subtle*."

"Who wants to be subtle?" Meg scoffed. "Subtle is a waste of everyone's time. If we would all just say what we mean, think of how many misunderstandings could be avoided."

"Is that so?" Eve leaned forward on her desk, an arch look in her eye. "Then why haven't you told Lucien that you melt into a puddle at the merest glimpse of him?"

"It hasn't come up," Meg replied pertly, then let out a long sigh. "Mostly because he's never spoken to me. Not that I insist upon conversation. I'd be perfectly satisfied if all he wants to do with me is—"

Eve slapped her hands over her ears. "I'm a le Duc now! We cannot talk that way about my *brother*-in-law."

Meg grinned back unrepentantly. It was good to be jocular with her best friend again. No, it was *wonderful*. Over the past fortnight, they'd barely seen each other, except at the wedding.

Not that Eve had cut old friends out of her life the moment she became a Proper Married Woman. The opposite; not a day went by without a note inviting Meg to join the happy duo for a supper here or a glass of wine there. But what kind of friend would Meg be if she inserted herself into a newlywed couple's private time together, just because Meg was lonely?

Setting up a new office, however, was exactly the sort of thing Meg excelled at. Although she liked to pretend there was nothing more in her head than the image of Lucien le Duc in tight buckskins—well, that and an abiding love for good chocolate—the truth was, Meg was a born organizer. She loved the late nights she'd spent helping set up the type for the quarterly Gazette. She loved helping her cousins manage milking times at the family dairy. She even loved doing occasional odd tasks around the castle.

Granted, none of those endeavors incurred a salary of any sort, but Meg had just enough funds to squeak by. She liked her life, just as it was. What else did she need?

"Congratulations again," she told Eve seriously. "You deserve this. *All* of this. True love *and* your dream of journalism come true."

"A new edition every month instead of every three months." Eve's expression was still filled with awe. "And I can write whatever I want."

"The current issue is your most popular yet." Meg lifted a copy from one of the many stacks. "Subscribers expected the traditional big Christmas edition, and you gave them that and so much more. Everyone in the whole village must have purchased theirs by now."

"Everyone everywhere," Eve admitted with a smile. "We had to reprint twice to fill all the requests from tourists." She tilted her head. "What about you?"

"I have three copies," Meg answered without hesitation. She always bought at least that many. One to read, one to save, and one for the castle library upstairs.

"I don't mean the Gazette. You helped me

to set up the type; you know what's in it." Eve crossed her arms. "I meant, what about you getting everything you ever wanted, too?"

Meg set down the newspaper.

"I already have everything I could ever want," she answered lightly. "A brilliant and talented bosom friend, who lets me spoil her dog. I share a home with my cousin and her husband, who are the kindest people in England. And we live in a beautiful mountaintop village that celebrates Christmastide all year round. I'm the luckiest person I know."

"You could be even luckier," Eve insisted. "What if you took a husband?"

"Good God." Meg groaned. "Please tell me you haven't turned into one of *those* already. I thought Old Married Lady syndrome wasn't supposed to start until five or six years in."

Eve's mouth fell open. "I'm not—"

"You were perfectly happy without a man in your life until Sébastien came along," Meg reminded her.

"And then I became happi*er*." Eve lifted her chin. "It could happen to you, too."

"I have plenty of opportunities for happiness." Meg pointed a finger toward the ceiling. "Do you know how many well-favored tourists pass through the castle's guest chambers every week?"

"You deserve a *lifetime* of happiness." Eve frowned. "Not just a night or two here and there."

"To be fair..." Meg wiggled her brows. "They tend to be very good nights."

Besides, she knew better than to risk her heart. Some people were lucky enough to find something which lasted forever, but Meg was not one of those people.

If life had taught her anything, it was that as soon as she was comfortable and content, something would happen to snatch it all away. It was much better not to pine for things one could not have in the first place. *Change* was the most dangerous thing of all.

Eve sighed. "If you want to be a scandalous spinster for the rest of your life—"

"I do," Meg assured her. She leaned a hip onto the corner of Eve's desk. "Highly recommended over the regular sort of spinster. You get all the best bits of having a man in your life without having to actually have a man in your life."

Eve narrowed her eyes. "Didn't you tell me you could stare at a man like Lucien le Duc for the rest of eternity?"

"I've been staring at his brooding deliciousness every day since I moved here six years ago without needing a leg-shackle, thank you very much. Besides, that's a terrible example. He despises everything English, and I'm... oh, right. *English*."

"No one could despise you," Eve said staunchly. "Although you're right; Lucien was a bad example. He'll be going back to France soon."

Meg couldn't hide her skepticism. "I don't think 'soon' means what you think it means. He's been planning to leave for as long as I can remember."

"The war just ended." Eve softened her voice. "He has a ticket. His ship sails on the sixth of January."

Meg's chest tightened. Of course Eve would know. News was her job, and she was part of the le Duc family now.

"Well, figs." Meg let out a disappointed sigh. "Glimpses of the devil-duke are one of the highlights of my day."

"Lucien is not a devil duke," Eve scolded her. "Didn't you read page four? He's a *Christmas* duke."

Meg gasped dramatically. "That means... this is my last chance for an extremely wicked

Christmas miracle!"

Eve covered her face with her hands. "That is not how miracles work."

"You have too many rules." Meg leapt up from the corner of Eve's desk. "You also have a lot of work to do, and I've interrupted enough. If you have extra time before you leave for home, I'll be upstairs in the library."

Eve grinned. "Torrid novels, I presume?"

"Is any other kind worth reading?" With a wink, Meg slipped out of her friend's new office and made her way up the castle's stone staircase to the public lending library.

Although Meg lived with her cousins, Allan and Jemima were out in the dairy from dawn until dusk, and the tiny cottage felt empty without them. Most days, there was nothing to do to help. Meg had already improved collection and delivery, and the farm had plenty of dairy maids. At least she could feel good about paying for her lodging. Jemima had offered the spare bedchamber free of charge, but Meg refused to be a burden. Not when she'd finally found a home.

Over time, she'd come to spend most of her days on the castle grounds because that was where the people were. Though winter was the busiest season, tourists flocked to beautiful Cressmouth year-round. The rolling hills of evergreens, the parks and the sleigh rides, the free meals offered thrice daily in the castle's grand public dining hall...

Who would want to live anywhere else?

CHAPTER 2

*L*ucien le Duc could not wait to go back home to France.

He was the second-best black-smith in a twenty-mile circumference, and he was tired of toiling every day before a scalding hot forge. Lucien could have become the *first*-best blacksmith if he could commu-nicate with his clients in their language, but English exhausted him even more than the forge.

His brother Sébastien's grease-stained hand poked out from under a mangled cabri-olet. "Can you hand me—"

Lucien passed him a vise and a hammer.

When they'd first emigrated here in the midst of a revolution, his *petit frère* Bastien had been too young to build carriages and smelt iron. He and their *petite sœur* Désirée had spent their days inside their uncle's cottage, hunched over children's books borrowed from the castle library.

Lucien, on the other hand, had been fifteen. A man, in his mind. When Uncle Jasper put him to work, Lucien wasn't resentful. He'd been *desperate* for something important to do. Anything at all to keep his trembling hands busy, and distract his mind from his terrified parents' final words before the crowd had grabbed them and—

"Can it be mended?" the cabriolet's owner fretted for the third time in a quarter of an hour.

Lucien pierced him with his infamous smiting glare. No one was a better blacksmith than Bastien. If he said he could do something, he did it. The careless driver would receive his ridiculous summer carriage back as soon as Bastien deemed it safe, and not a moment earlier.

The man shrank back against the wall with both palms raised. "I'll wait."

Lucien turned back to his post, where one of the village sleighs awaited winter maintenance.

Well, technically, it wasn't Lucien's post

anymore, *n'est-ce pas?* After years of working at his uncle's side, then many more years of running the smithy alongside his brother after their uncle's health forced him into retirement, Lucien could retire, too. Huzzah.

To some, four-and-thirty might seem a young age to retire. To Lucien, the years had been interminable.

He and his siblings had not been born to a humble family of country blacksmiths, but rather to a long line of blue-blooded French *noblesse*. Their family had possessed a grand chateau, endless coffers, a sprawling vineyard… He and his siblings had been destined to a life of leisure, just like their parents, and their grandparents before them.

And then: the war.

Lucien pushed those thoughts away, just as he always did. He would not dwell on the past, but concentrate on the future. What had been stolen from them would soon be returned. Not their childhood or their parents, but the land of their birth. Their place in society. The life they were always meant to lead. As soon as the war ended, he'd petitioned the government to restore their lost property. *Grâce à* distant familial connections to the new king, Lucien was certain the answer would be yes.

After paying off their debts and ensuring Uncle Jasper would be safe and comfortable, he and his siblings could finally return home.

Except, Désirée was now married with children, living in a fine house just up the road. And the smithy's new owners had signed a generous contract making Bastien the lead foreman. All profit, no expenses.

Bastien had also married. He didn't *need* to go home. He and Désirée had made new homes here in Cressmouth.

Lucien was the only one left who didn't belong.

A coach-and-four pulled to a halt in front of the smithy, and a gaggle of well-dressed young ladies in feathered hats and fur muffs tumbled out onto the frost-tipped gravel.

"Oh!" gasped one. "That must be a le Duc brother. My, are they handsome."

"Are you Lucien?" her friend called out boldly. "Or Sébastien?"

Their companions giggled and fluttered their eyelashes expectantly.

Lucien glared at them all.

"It's Lucien," the bold one whispered with confidence. "See how he smolders?"

He turned his back to them and resumed his work on the sleigh.

It wasn't that he disliked young ladies. Lucien enjoyed ladies very, very much. He did not, however, enjoy looking like a fool in front of them.

Stammering out mispronounced words in jumbled grammar did not behoove an erstwhile aristocrat. He'd much rather be judged surly than stupid, and he definitely wouldn't put himself in any position that displayed a weakness.

Between his potent glares and his reclusiveness with anyone who wasn't family, Lucien had managed to stay out of the English villagers' way.

Until that bloody article in the bloody Christmas Gazette.

Lucien's name had always been known to his neighbors—after all, theirs was the only smithy for miles—but now that his new sister-in-law had printed a front page article fawning over the smithy's integral role in the community and the le Duc brothers who ran it, every tourist passing in or out of the village stopped for a quick peek. He half-expected some of them to whip out a sketchbook or dash off a quick watercolor to immortalize the moment.

He was *not* a curiosity. He was a man. This was a smithy, not a circus—and certainly not a *boutique* wherein to obtain a temporary Frenchman, as some of these English women seemed to think. The only marriage mart Lucien was interested in was the one back at home. *French* ladies, who shared his history and his culture and his language.

And if he wasn't going to court these silly chits, he certainly didn't plan to *ravish* them, for God's sake. He did not wish to be a notch on anyone's bedpost, nor did he desire to add to his own. He was a *gentleman*. He might not look like it here, hunched in scratched boots and charred leather gloves, but he would be a proper gentleman again once his birthright was restored.

When he found the mademoiselle he wished to spend the rest of his life with, Lucien intended to deserve her. Meanwhile, he saw no advantage to wasting anyone's time.

"Pardon me," one of the ladies called out. "Can you tell us which cottage belongs to the Duke of Nottingvale?"

Non. Lucien did not have all the right words, and wouldn't disclose someone else's information even if he did. Not that he was surprised to hear them ask. They were far from the first.

Nottingvale's annual Christmastide house parties were almost as famous in Cressmouth as winter plays in the amphitheater or ice-skating on the castle pond... but much more exclusive. Only a select few received an invitation. A handful from the *beau monde*, and a handful who were not. Never the same guests twice.

Never the le Ducs at all.

He wasn't bitter, Lucien reminded himself. If he had stayed part of the nobility, he wouldn't invite blacksmiths to his lavish fêtes either. It was just... He wasn't *meant* to be a blacksmith. None of his siblings were. They were supposed to be a "better." Just like Nottingvale, important because they were born to be.

Not fleeting tourist curiosities because that was how far they'd managed to fall.

"Good afternoon, ladies," came an unctuous male voice. "I'm the smithy's new coordinator to the public, and I'll be happy to answer any questions or give you a private tour, if you'd like."

17

Lucien poked his head up from over the sleigh in disbelief.

Some fop with clothes even more pretentious than Lucien's dandy brother was standing in the middle of the group of women. Who the devil was that?

Lucien stalked over to the cabriolet and kicked Bastien's boot.

"*Qui est cet homme?*" he demanded.

"He's cordnerer pufflic," came the garbled reply, likely because Bastien had screws or a wrench between his teeth.

"I heard what he *said.*" Lucien dropped into a crouch to glare at his younger brother. "What the deuce does it *mean?*"

Bastien pulled the wrench from his teeth and sighed. "It means, thanks to the Gazette, the smithy is now one of Cressmouth's top attractions. The Harpers have employed a go-between to handle the influx of tourists."

Lucien's head jerked back. "They're *paying* someone to deflect distractions so everyone else can work? They must be furious."

"They're delighted." Bastien shrugged. "High prestige comes with higher prices. Two new apprentices will start in the morning. Lads from town. That article is the best thing that could have happened to the smithy."

Lucien stared back at him, speechless.

Bastien was right. Lucien might abhor the unwelcome attention, but the smithy was thriving. Cressmouth was thriving. *Bastien* was thriving. And Lucien was… redundant.

He didn't belong here, either.

Without another word, he rose to his feet, placed his gloves and leather apron on their hooks upon the wall, and walked out of the smithy.

Lucien didn't have a contract with the Harpers. He wasn't being paid to work. He'd been paid to sell. Why the devil was he toiling in a loud, dirty smithy when he could be living the life of indolence he'd spent the past two decades fighting for?

Because that was his brother under the cabriolet, that's why. Because his father's last words had been *be the man I expect you to be* and his mother's last words had been *take care of your siblings*.

Even if they didn't need him anymore.

He pushed open the door to the cottage and stalked toward his private chamber. He stopped when he glimpsed Uncle Jasper in the drawing room, one gouty leg propped up on a stool and his balding head tucked against the side of a wingback chair.

Lucien didn't ask, *Comment va ton pied?* because the answer was obvious. Uncle Jasper was in pain. There was little to relieve it, save for cold compresses and a cup of willow bark tea. Lucien turned away from his private quarters and headed to the kitchen instead.

In no time, he had cool compresses on his uncle's swollen leg and a fresh pot of tea at his side.

"Thank you," Uncle Jasper murmured. "That last pot had gone cold."

Lucien frowned. He'd been in the smithy all day; there hadn't been time to make pots of tea. How would Uncle Jasper...

Oh. Lucien tightened his jaw. They weren't alone in the cottage anymore. His sister-in-law lived there, too. She must have tended to Jasper before leaving for the castle. Lucien was now just as superfluous inside his house as he was out in the smithy.

The worst part was, he couldn't even be irritated. He was *grateful* to Eve for taking care of his uncle. *Grateful* to the Harpers for the windfall that had given their family financial solvency. *Grateful* that his siblings had found love and homes and happiness.

Lucien slumped into the chair opposite his

uncle's footstool and rubbed his face with his hands.

There were no more ties keeping him in England, but the same wasn't true for everyone. He had been a selfish blackguard to hope Bastien and Désirée would want to come with him when he knew they'd be happier here without him.

His siblings didn't remember France like he did. They'd been eight and ten when their parents were killed. Lucien had been a few scant years away from being treated as an adult in charge of his own life. Bastien had been thinking of wooden trucks and Désirée of porcelain dolls, but Lucien was already joining his parents on trips here and visits there, dance instructors and university tours, preparing him for life he was going to live in just a few years. That was the world he yearned to go back to. The life he longed to have for the first time. The one his parents had died trying to provide for him.

He owed it to them even more than he owed it to himself. Lucien had given up his childhood, given up every hour of his life to provide for his family, but it didn't compare to the ultimate sacrifice his parents had made.

Be the man I expect you to be.

I will, sir. I promise.

He patted Jasper's liver-spotted hand and rose to his feet.

Once Lucien had land and a house back home in France, he'd find a way to bring Jasper over if his uncle wished to visit, or even to stay. All Lucien had to do was make it six more weeks. Twelfth Night would be his last day in England. His last day of being *lesser*. He was going to prove he belonged in the world his parents wanted to give him, and never have to fight again.

When he reached his chamber, three books wrapped in twine sat on his side table.

English books. Childish English books meant for children. No doubt a nudge from his sister.

Lucien opened the folded note laying on top:

I thought of you.
These are from the castle library.
Don't stop practicing just because I'm not there.
You can do it.
Désirée

Maybe he could and maybe he couldn't. Not starting until he was an adult had not helped matters. Neither did his unwillingness to display his obvious inferiority in front of others. For a while, Lucien had muddled through anyway. Now he no longer needed to. No matter what happened with his petition to the courts, he had a one-way ticket back to France. Back to where he belonged.

Lucien scooped up the books and walked them outside to the winding road leading up to the castle. Just like he wasn't necessary anymore, neither were these books.

He ignored the curious looks as he strode in through the castle's busy reception hall and up the stone spiral stairs. Most of the villagers came to the castle several times a week for meals or entertainment. Lucien was an unusual sight. He rarely came closer than the public park, where his new niece and nephew liked to play. Until he sold the smithy, Lucien hadn't had time to try to fit in. Now that he had time, he no longer needed to bother.

He stepped across the threshold and into the library.

Empty. Perfect. He hadn't wanted anyone to witness him returning books meant for babies.

Maybe what he ought to pick up were a few things in French. Was there a latest novel everyone would be raving about? A fascinating biography? Advances in wine production and the cultivation of grapes? He stepped around the corner... and crashed directly into a young woman emerging from between two tall shelves.

Her book went flying.

His books went flying.

She flailed for balance.

He caught her.

Gray-blue eyes met his and widened.

He sighed and summoned his best English. "You wonder... if I am... the local blacksmith…"

Her eyes glinted with mischief. "I'm actually wondering what else you can do with those big, strong hands."

He let her go.

She placed the back of her wrist against her forehead and dramatically slumped against his chest as though she had just swooned.

Her eyes were still open. And twinkling wickedly.

Lucien had absolutely no idea how a gentleman should respond. So he froze. Her hair smelled like lilacs. An errant curl tickled his jaw. He had a feeling she knew it.

She pushed away from his chest and burst out laughing. "I've been dying to be alone with you for six long years. I thought I'd imagined every possible way it might happen, but you've just exceeded my every expectation. You even let me nuzzle against your chest for the briefest of moments. It was just as warm and hard and muscular as I dreamed it would be."

He stared at her helplessly. The more she talked, the less he knew what to do with her.

"Here." She knelt to the floor. "Let me retrieve your books."

"*No*," he barked, but it was too late.

A Little Pretty Pocket-Book was already in her hand.

She blinked at the title. "Interesting choice. I prefer gothic intrigue, and a shameless lack of virtue, but I suppose this could also... No, it probably couldn't." She handed him back his books.

"Who *are* you?" he managed.

But of course he knew who she was. Not her name, but her face. The village was much too small for even a recluse like Lucien not to recognize other locals. He'd glimpsed this black-haired beauty several times in the company of his new sister-in-law. Her generous curves and blue-gray eyes were impossible to miss. Nor could anyone mistake her habit of throwing back her head with a laugh so shockingly loud, so unabashedly delighted, so enticingly infectious, that even a marble statue would be tempted to smile back.

What he hadn't realized was that she'd been watching him, too.

"I'm Meg." She dipped an impressively graceful curtsey.

He waited.

She added no additional information.

He cleared his throat. "Meg…"

"Meg, of the Christmas Megs." She smiled brightly, then fluttered her eyes heavenward. "If you must have all the boring details, I am Miss Margaret Church, cousin to Mr. and Mrs. Allan Farrell of the local dairy, and yes, I live there, too. Eve insists on saying 'Margaret' just to needle me, but friends can call me Meg."

"Are we friends?" he asked doubtfully.

"Oh, do I get to decide? In that case, yes. We are most definitely friends. I'm Meg, and you're… may I call you Luc?"

"No."

She tapped her cheek. "Lucien, then. But wouldn't it be fun if we all had a one-syllable name? Meg, Luc, Eve, Beau—"

He crossed his arms. "My brother's name… is Bastien."

"Ah, but you knew who I was talking about, didn't you? Yet I see your point. If everyone used a single-syllable nickname, it would become monotonous. Maybe Eve has it right, and I should be Margaret after all. Well, too late for us. You're a friend who calls me Meg. I'll have to save 'Margaret' for the next rugged blacksmith I collide with at the library."

Lucien wished he knew a polite way to say *Do you always talk this much?* in English.

But he wasn't here to be polite to English people. He was here to rid himself of English nonsense that he had no interest in reading.

Mademoiselle Church either took deep pleasure in being shocking, or she had no idea how scandalous her behavior actually was. A gentleman would walk away, so as not to find himself embroiled in scandal himself.

And he would leave. Any second now.

He narrowed his eyes. She was no debutante. Not just for lack of manners, but because Lucien took her age to be at least five-and-twenty. A beautiful spinster living in someone else's humble country farm would imply Mademoiselle Church was an impoverished cousin relying on family charity. A poor relation to a *dairy maid*. Leagues beneath the caliber of well-bred aristocratic young ladies Lucien would be associating with once he returned to France.

No doubt she saw that damnable article in the Cressmouth Gazette, realized his family was no longer as poor as they'd been, and determined that a blacksmith would be a step up from her current circumstances. Well, he wasn't interested. Not in her, or any English-woman. She would have to find some other mark to bat those long eyelashes at.

He opened his mouth to tell her so.

"No, no, don't stop now." She fanned her neck. "I *love* the way you glower. I have no idea what you're thinking and really it doesn't matter, because if you told me, all the mystery would go away. When you cross those big, strong arms over that wide chest and narrow those piercing chocolate-brown eyes to slits, it feels as though you've smited an entire room with the power of your thoughts. It comes across positively devilish." She lowered her voice. "I adore anything wicked."

He glared at her.

She clutched her chest. "Oh dear, my bosom... it's *heaving*. And my nether regions..." A giggle escaped her throat. "Does that phrase make you think of the Batavian Republic, too, or am I the only one? 'Nether regions,' the Netherlands... I always wonder why authors ruin a perfectly good licentious scene with words that sound like vague references to international diplomacy. Why can't a woman just say that what she'd *really* like a man to do is—"

"*Stop*," Lucien choked, his buckskins suddenly uncomfortable. He would never be able to hear news about Holland again without thinking of Mademoiselle Church and her nether regions.

She knew *exactly* how shocking she was being, he realized. She was doing it on purpose. Poking at him with her words the way she claimed he "smote" others with his eyes.

He wouldn't stand for it.

Lucien turned his back—a cut direct was rude, but still well within a gentleman's arsenal—and shoved his books onto the closest shelf.

"How was the *Pretty Pocket-Book*, by the

by?" she asked, as if genuinely interested. "Should I give it a try?"

He spun back to her and... now that he knew what it did to her nether regions, he certainly couldn't *glare*, but what else was he supposed to do with his face when he didn't know the right words to say?

"You didn't read it?" she said in surprise, then gave a little shrug. "To be honest, I probably wouldn't have, either. I make fun of the vague descriptions in my favorite books, but I would cry if they weren't in there. I'm hoping *Fanny Hill* isn't afraid to say what it means." She held her book out toward him. "Here. You read it first, and let me know if it's something I might like."

He would do no such thing. He couldn't if he wanted to. *Fanny Hill* was a novel. Lucien could barely make it through the eight-page Cressmouth Gazette. Not that he would admit such a failure aloud. Better her to think him scandalized than stupid.

Lucien tried to assume his haughtiest, most condescending expression of disapproval.

His neck and ears flushed with heat to spite him.

"You can't *read* it?" she breathed in wonder, then shook her head. "Of course you can't read it. You're French."

"French people… can read!" he ground out in offense.

"Yes, yes, obviously I meant because it's in English, which is not nearly as romantic as French." Her eyes narrowed. "I'll wager French novelists aren't dipping their quills in ink only to waste perfectly good parchment with phrases like 'redheaded champion' and 'prurient ivory mounds.' But when all one has is English…" Her breath caught. "Oh, I'll teach you! There are *so* many good books on these shelves. You've no idea what you're missing. Come, sit by the fire and let me assess your level of—"

"*No*," he growled.

Lucien turned and stalked from the library without another word. He didn't need English, he didn't need Miss Church, and he definitely did not need her pity.

If he were fluent, he would have told her so.

CHAPTER 3

*M*eg lay in the center of her bed and sighed, doubly disappointed with *Fanny Hill*.

First, because if she hadn't experienced several of the referenced sensations firsthand, she'd have no idea how to parse many of its florid metaphors. Second, because the finer points of crimson swords in moist caves was precisely the sort of conversation she'd prefer to be having with Lucien le Duc, rather than alone in her head. Her stomach twisted.

She'd insulted him; she could see that now. Although she still wasn't certain whether the slight stemmed from suggesting Lucien didn't know English or the presumption that he would *want* to. If Meg possessed an enormous private library filled with gripping French literature, she wouldn't bother with the castle's English selection either.

She tossed the book aside. The sun was setting, which meant Jemima would be coming in from the dairy and Meg wouldn't have to be alone with her thoughts anymore.

"Thank God," she muttered.

Meg rolled off her bed and hopped over to the looking-glass. The side she'd been lying on was now an impressive mishmash of wrinkles. It didn't matter. She'd be chatting with her cousin, not taking her curtsey to High Society. Besides, she didn't have a better dress to change into. If most of Meg's meager income didn't go to rent, perhaps she could afford a new gown, but the best she could do was keep replacing frayed lace or worn hems on the items she already owned.

Luckily, Jemima loved her just as she was.

When Meg heard the front door open, she raced out of her bedchamber to greet her cousin. Moving to Cressmouth had been one of the hardest upheavals in Meg's life, but Jemima and Allan had been a blessing. More than a blessing—a *constant*. Exactly what Meg needed in a time when everything was upside-down. Not only had they helped her start over, they'd given her what she craved most: family, friends, *roots*.

"Mrs. Farrell," Meg called out. "My, you look fetching. The wind has given your cheeks a remarkable glow. Come, join me in the sitting room so you can dwarf me with your beauty. How were the cows today? There's a violinist at the castle tonight. Shall we go and practice country dances? Or should we just partake of the complimentary mulled wine?"

Jemima burst out laughing and threw her arm about Meg's waist. "Poor thing. Eve's at her new post, isn't she? You must be positively starved for conversation."

"How do you do it?" Meg groaned. "When the Gazette only consumed Eve once a quarter, we had plenty of opportunity to debate and philosophize. How can you spend all day with cattle? Granted, I don't speak their language, but cows don't seem like ideal verbal sparring partners."

"She doesn't spend all day talking to cows," said a gruff male voice. "She spends all day talking to me."

Jemima sent a fond expression over her shoulder as Allan walked in the door.

"That's what husbands are for," she protested, then turned back to Meg. "You—"

"If you tell me I should get one, I swear I shall scream," Meg interrupted. "I *like* being in charge of my own life. The freedoms of spinsterhood disappear when one is no longer a spinster. As long as I remain unwed, I have *rights*."

She'd *had* a guardian once.

Never again.

Jemima looped her arm through Allan's and rested her head on his shoulder, eyes twinkling. "Marriage has his advantages."

Meg sniffed. "Name one."

Jemima and Allan exchanged a knowing glance.

"Fair enough," Meg grumbled. "Name another one."

"That's actually something we'd like to talk to you about." Allan led his wife to the sofa and motioned for Meg to take the chair opposite.

She did so with trepidation.

"Is it the wrinkles?" she asked. "I know about the wrinkles. I borrowed a new book and I was only going to read the first chapter, but then the next thing I knew—"

"It's not the wrinkles," Jemima assured her. "I smell like cow. I can abide a few wrinkles."

"What she cannot abide is smelling like cow," Allan said meaningfully.

Meg frowned. "You're going to sell the dairy?"

"We can't sell the dairy. It's our only income."

"You're going to have a dairy without cows?"

"We're keeping the cows." Jemima leaned forward, eyes shining. "Meg, I'm pregnant."

Pregnant.

Meg flew off her seat and wrapped her arms about them both. "This is the best news I've heard in my life! Congratulations, both of you. I cannot *wait* to be an aunt. I can be an aunt even if I'm a cousin, can't I? I'm going to be the best aunt a baby could ever have. Or maybe the worst. Does spoiling make me good or bad? Cressmouth is always so cold. I'll buy wool tomorrow so I can knit a little hat for the baby."

Jemima pulled away, laughing. "You don't know how to knit."

"I've several months to learn, don't I?" Meg pointed out. "What else am I to do with my time?"

Jemima's smile fell. This time, the glance she shared with her husband was not playful, but anguished.

Sudden fear clogged Meg's throat. Her muscles tightened. "What is it?"

"We love you very much," Jemima said quickly. Meg's sense of dread only intensified. "And we absolutely want you to be an everyday part of our son or daughter's life. But this cottage only has two rooms. The one you're in now was always meant to be a nursery one day, if we ever needed it."

"And now you need it." Meg's words were almost too soft to hear.

She knew better than to believe in something lasting forever. In *permanent*. In *home*. As soon as she had what she wanted, something always came to take it away. Her friends, her parents, her home. She'd been silly to believe that just because she found a new home, she'd ever be allowed to keep it.

"We know you don't have anywhere to go," Allan began gently.

This wasn't entirely true. Meg had some*where*. A tiny plot of empty land an ocean away. It was the only reminder she had left of everything she'd once had and lost, and it was utterly useless.

She didn't have enough money to travel, and even if she went, then what? There was no family there. No house to live in. No crops to eat. The only income Meg had was the few coins she earned from letting a neighbor graze his cattle on her grass. For all Meg knew, that was destroying the land—yet she couldn't afford to stop. Without that revenue, she'd have nothing at all.

If her small income was barely enough to get by here in Cressmouth, she'd be even worse off anywhere else. At least with the castle's public offerings to supplement the villagers' incomes...

"I'll find something," she assured them. "Something close by, I promise. Just a stone's throw away. I'll be fine."

"There's no need for haste," Jemima said quickly, patting her still flat stomach. "We just thought you should know, so you would have time to... plan."

Meg nodded. She was good at planning, at making things work and making do, at being boisterous to hide the flailing inside.

She'd had a lifetime of practice.

CHAPTER 4

*L*ucien yanked weeds from the family garden with more force than usual.

Not that anything was "usual" anymore. Until his *petite sœur* had left home and got married, Lucien had never even visited the family garden. In fact, he distinctly remembered forbidding Désirée from working in the dirt because it was unseemly for a lady of her soon-to-be-restored stature.

She hadn't listened. The family had to eat. And now that Lucien could finally afford to visit the village market and purchase everything in sight, here he was stabbing at frozen soil with a trowel because he had absolutely nothing better to do with his time.

The smithy was overrun with clients and employees alike. The Harpers' new "representative to the public" had hung sprigs of mistletoe and boughs of holly on every post and wall. His sister-in-law was in the drawing room playing *vingt-et-un* with Uncle Jasper.

And Lucien... was out back behind the house, stabbing at a dead garden. Demoted from *head of household* to *irrelevant*. He yanked up his gloves. After years of refusing to accept their temporary lodgings as "home," now that everything had changed, he could no longer deny that a *home* was exactly what it had become.

He missed the smithy, blast it all. Missed it and hated it. He missed being the one his uncle depended upon, the one his *petit frère* and *petite sœur* looked up to, the one who spent thousands of sleepless nights worrying about making the best possible decisions for the well-being of his family. The responsibility had been suffocating. But he'd loved it, because he loved them. Protecting his siblings was more than a duty. They were part of his soul.

And now they didn't need him.

He should be thrilled. What better sign could there be that he'd fulfilled the promise he'd made to their parents? His siblings were safe and happy, in love and beloved.

They also weren't going anywhere on the sixth of January. When Epiphany came, Lucien would have to sail for home without them.

He touched the waistcoat pocket that hid the tickets. Bastien had purchased boat passage believing the two brothers would make the trip side-by-side. Now he was working fewer hours and earning greater dividends than ever at the smithy. His wife Eve had gone from being an unpaid workhorse on her father's gazette to being in charge of the castle's public communications *and* well-compensated. They would still visit, Bastien said. All of them.

It wouldn't be the same, but it would have to be enough.

Lucien would fulfill his final promise and restore his siblings' birthright. It would be there if and when they wanted it, but more importantly, all the opportunities that had been taken from them would be there for future generations. Lucien's children would never be laughed at, pointed at, or whispered about because they were *too different* from everyone else. They would grow up in a single, happy home, speak the same language as their neighbors, be treated with compassion and respect.

They would never have to doubt their place in the world. They'd be born into the life Lucien's parents had wanted to give their own children.

Which meant, of course, that as soon as the family assets were restored, Lucien's next priority would be securing an appropriate bride.

An image of laughing blue-gray eyes flashed through his mind.

He shook his head. Could there be a less suitable woman than Mademoiselle Church? No wonder she was a spinster. She was brash and boisterous, inappropriate and ill-bred, wicked and witty, surprisingly clever...

"Nether regions" reminded her of the *Batavian Republic?* Why would *anything* remind her of the Batavian Republic? "Redheaded champions" should make her think of... cow teats, perhaps. Something innocent. Didn't she live in a dairy?

What's more, how had she seen through him so clearly? She'd talked through the entire encounter and yet somehow managed to glean information he'd spent years concealing.

He hadn't really let her nuzzle his chest, had he? Lucien rubbed the back of his neck. He'd *known* it wasn't a real swoon, and yet he'd already caught her in his arms. It was too late. What was a gentleman supposed to do with a damsel in distress, even if her weak knees were the result of playacting? His flesh heated.

Part of him couldn't help but wonder what their encounter might have been like if their fortunes were different. If Lucien were a lord, and she *une dame*. Would he have been appalled by her scandalous behavior and given her the cut direct in a fancy ballroom? Or would he have waltzed with her beneath a crystal chandelier and out through a garden door in order to steal a kiss beneath the moonlight?

ourists might find it too cold outside for a picnic, but Cressmouth's residents didn't let a minor detail like the weather keep them cooped inside on a sunny winter's day.

Meg, her cousin Jemima, and a hundred tourists and neighbors dotted the castle park. Some had come for a stroll, some had come to skate on the frozen lake, and the most intrepid of all... tossed a thick blanket onto the hard ground from which to sit back and comment to each other about everything around them.

"Look, there's Gloria." Meg gestured toward their friend. "I wonder if she's entertaining tourists this evening. Her Star Walks are so much fun."

Jemima tilted her head toward the village jeweler. "Did you see Angelica? She looks *stunning*. The way that cluster of pearls stand out against her gorgeous dark hair and skin... If I had money, I'd give it all to her so she could fashion me something with sparkles to distract from my soon-to-be huge belly."

"Your future belly will make you even more beautiful than you already are," Meg assured her cousin. "But if you want a distraction, I'll knit a hat for you, too."

A streak of gray atop the hill caught their eye. The corner of Jemima's mouth quirked. "Tiny Tim looks... wide awake."

They both watched in amusement as the castle's indefatigable pygmy goat leapt around the park in hircine delight.

Meg tried not to be melancholy at the idea of no longer living with her cousin. She loved spontaneous moments like these. Her throat grew thick. She was leaving the cottage, but it wasn't as if she was leaving Cressmouth, Meg told herself firmly. She'd still see her cousin every day. Jemima just wouldn't be right down the hall.

Perhaps Meg would spend more time here, on the castle grounds. There was always a surfeit of tourists eager to chat with the locals. Sure, their camaraderie would last for a week or two at best and a moment or two at worst, but if Meg was destined to gradually lose everyone she cared about anyway, what was the difference? At least she'd still be in a place she considered home.

"Do you miss France?" asked Jemima, her gaze soft.

"No," Meg said flatly. Usually her answers tended to the verbose, but when it came to France, there wasn't much Meg wanted to say.

She'd been dragged there against her will at age ten. She'd *liked* their comfortable home in Berwick-upon-Tweed, *loved* her pretty bedchamber and her neighborhood full of friends.

We'll come back, her mother had promised. *You'll make new friends*, her father had said. Some cousin of a cousin was involved in an investment arrangement that was going to make them all wealthy beyond their wildest dreams.

The first thing to lose had been the carriage. No more trips into town; no more Sunday promenades. Then her mother's jewels. Earrings, necklaces, wedding ring. Then the house. They moved into the attic of a new business associate. Just for a while. Just until they got back on their feet.

Then Father became ill. Something about the coal in the mines filling his lungs with black dust, day after day. He wasn't supposed to be *in* the mines, Meg had protested. He was an investor, not a miner. Yes, but that had been Before. Father wasn't an investor anymore. He'd spent every penny they had, save for a small plot of land that had been in Mother's family for generations, and now formed the entirety of Meg's dowry.

Not that there was much chance of meeting eligible gentlemen. Meg spent her days up in the attic sewing noble ladies' luxurious gowns with her mother, and a half dozen other impoverished women in the neighborhood. They wouldn't suffer like this if the world were more equitable, they said. No wonder there was a revolution in the streets. Some people were born to dine with silver spoons, and others were born to choke on black dust and sew with bleeding fingers.

"I'm not going back," was all she said aloud.

She knew what awaited her there. *Nothing.* Precisely what had awaited her parents. She'd sobbed on their graves during her one free day each month and swore to never fall for someone else's grandiose ideas ever again.

"I'm sorry." Jemima's expression was stricken. "I should not have brought it up."

Meg forced a sunny smile. "You should bring up anything you like. Of course it was on your mind. You worry about where I'll go, now that I can't stay with you. But you needn't worry. I always find a way. I found my way here to you, didn't I?"

A voyage which had involved stowing away on a passenger ship and being consigned to the scullery the moment she was found out. Above deck was a ballroom, or at least that was how the stomping feet and muffled music sounded when it trickled through below.

By then, Meg had been long out of the old attic, but the life that awaited her wasn't much better. She was too terrified of being taken advantage of to sell her plot of land outright, yet its humble earnings were not enough to live a comfortable, respectable life. Meg had given up on respectability years before, but she hadn't given up on putting down roots and being close to her family. She never would.

She gave Jemima's hand a squeeze. "It will

work out, cousin. You cannot get rid of me that easily."

"Oh, I could get rid of you if I wanted to." Jemima's eyes twinkled. "All I'd have to say is, 'Look, there's Lucien le Duc' and you'd forget I even existed."

Meg dropped her jaw in faux outrage. "Unfair! I am not nearly so shallow as—"

"No, *look*." Jemima tapped Meg's leg. "He's ten yards behind you. And he's *not brooding*."

Meg shook her head. "He's always brooding."

"Not this time," Jemima insisted. "He looks… mystified?"

Meg turned to see for herself.

Jemima was right.

Lucien was leaning against a birch tree, arms folded over his broad chest, staring at Meg with an expression that could be best described as consternation.

Meg wiggled her fingers in a wave.

Lucien did not wave back.

"It's killing him not to glare," she whispered to Jemima. "I know why he's not brooding."

"Why?" Jemima whispered back.

"Because I told him his seductive sulks arouse me in my nether regions."

A snort escaped Jemima's nose and she fell onto the picnic blanket sideways in a fit of giggles. "The poor man! I thought that sort of thing was private information."

"Oh yes, I absolutely want him to become familiar with my privates," Meg answered with a straight face. "According to a very instructive book I'm reading, my 'womanly indraught' can offer 'sweetly soothing balmy titillation' to 'the maypole of a young giant.'"

Tears of laughter escaped Jemima's eyes. "Exactly how my mother explained it to me on my wedding night. She must have read the same book. I had no idea what she was going on about."

"It's a cipher," Meg agreed. Rather like Lucien le Duc. Just when she thought she was starting to understand him, he managed to surprise her.

When his nephew's trundling hoop escaped its stick and came barreling straight at Lucien, he did not freeze the lad in one of his infamous smiting glares. Faster than she'd ever seen anyone move, Lucien bent to snatch his own stick from the ground, pierced it through the hoop, and raced off with the trundling hoop with his niece and nephew shrieking in joy behind him.

The broodingest, scowliest, most infamous curmudgeon in Cressmouth was a good sport and great with children.

Meg reacted all the way to her nether regions.

"I can't believe he's leaving," she said with a groan. "Six years for him to speak to me... What are the chances of him plundering my mouth with punishing kisses between now and Epiphany?"

"Maybe you were too subtle," Jemima suggested. "Did you specifically *demand* to be plundered with punishing kisses? Men can't read women's minds, you know."

"I'll be clearer next time," Meg promised. "If he doesn't plunder me first, I'll turn into a plunderess myself."

"That's the spirit." Jemima patted Meg's knee. "Don't forget to rip his bodice open. Maybe fling his cravat aside dramatically for good measure."

"With my teeth," Meg agreed, pantomiming the action. "*Rawr.* Scowl at me again, sir! There go your buttons, too. Now prepare for sweetly soothing balmy titillation!"

Jemima wrinkled her nose. "It doesn't

sound very plunder-y. The first part was good, and then it lost steam."

"I'll improvise," Meg assured her. "I also have about six more chapters to read. Anything could happen. I'm taking copious notes."

"Good afternoon, ladies," came a low male voice.

Jemima and Meg started in unison and spun to face the speaker.

Bastien and Eve stood arm in arm, a pair of ice-skates dangling from their free hands.

"What were you two talking about?" he asked curiously.

"Er…" Meg said brightly. "Buttons?"

Eve rescued them by motioning toward the frozen water. "Want to take a turn about the pond with us? There are carts and skates to rent."

"No, thank you." Both Meg and Jemima shook their heads. Jemima, due to her happy condition. Meg, because she needed to mind her pennies now more than ever. Even the bread in her picnic basket had come from the castle buffet.

"Does Lucien skate?" she blurted out.

"I've never seen him do so," Bastien said slowly. "Then again, he was the one who told me pies would be free today, to welcome skaters to the lake."

Meg had seen the same article.

"He reads the *Cressmouth Gazette*?" she said incredulously.

Her best friend arched both brows.

"It's a lovely paper," Meg explained hurriedly. "An exceptional convergence of fine journalism and good taste. I just wouldn't think that Lucien…"

Good God, she *had* offended him. If he could read the Gazette, he'd have no need for children's books. There were a hundred other explanations. The man had a niece and nephew, didn't he? He was playing with the twins right now.

Her ears flushed with heat.

Eve frowned in concern. "What happened?"

"Among other conversational missteps," Meg mumbled, "I offered unsolicited English tutoring to your brother-in-law."

"He could use it," Bastien said without hesitation. "But he'd sooner throw himself off this mountain than admit it. He won't trust anyone but family with perceived weaknesses. And even then, Désirée was the only one he ever let try to help."

Meg heart thumped. She could understand being private. If she wouldn't discuss France with her own cousin, she could scarcely fault Lucien for refusing English lessons from a total stranger. It also put his deadly glares into perspective. By choosing not to communicate, he could wield his otherness like a weapon, rather than let others wound him by casting him aside.

"I suppose it doesn't matter," Eve said. "He won't need English when he goes back to France."

Meg straightened. "He won't come back, even for visits?"

"We're more likely to go and visit him there," Bastien explained. He exchanged a smile with his wife. "Our home is here in Cressmouth, but my history is still from France. Once Lucien is settled, perhaps we can spend winters with him."

"Summers," Eve corrected with an expression of shock. "You can't think to deprive our future children of Christmas in Cressmouth!"

"It's *always* Christmas in Cressmouth," Bastien pointed out. "How will they even know?"

Their teasing faded as Bastien and Eve made their way down to the frozen pond.

Meg wished she were half as confident about her future as everyone else seemed to be about their own. Jemima and Allan would be here, Lucien would be there, Bastien and Eve would divide their time between the two, and Meg...

Meg didn't even know where she'd be living a year from now.

"Don't make that face," Jemima said. "That face worries me."

"I'm just thinking maybe I oughtn't to plunder Lucien, after all." The occasional embrace of a passing tourist was one thing, but a torrid affair with her best friend's brother-in-law? Meg would be constantly tempted to ask about him, and tortured every time they mentioned his name and how much happier he was now that he was far away.

"If it's because he's a slow reader, I find that a very shallow reason," Jemima whispered. "And a missed opportunity for seeing the look on his face when you tear off his cravat with your teeth."

"It's not because he's a slow reader." Meg's chest constricted. "If you recall, I tried to help him with his English before I realized there was no chance on Earth that he would want my help."

"Anyone's help," Jemima corrected. "It didn't sound personal."

Meg caught sight of Mr. Thompson, the castle solicitor, out of the corner of her eye.

She jumped to her feet.

Jemima's eyes widened in alarm. "Where are you going?"

"What if Lucien doesn't *know* I'm helping?" Meg shook out her skirts. "I'll be back soon."

Quickly, before the solicitor could disappear into the castle, Meg raced to his side. "Mr. Thompson?"

"Yes, Miss Church?"

"Has the castle library already spent its annual budget on new books?"

"By November," Mr. Thompson answered, "normally that answer would be 'yes.' This year, however, we received a sizable literary donation from the Duke of Azureford. I'd have to review the ledgers to be certain, but I doubt we've touched much of the budget. Why? Is there a specific book you'd like me to order for you?"

A hundred desultory titles popped into Meg's mind at once. She pushed them away. The castle library had plenty of novels that she could read, torrid or otherwise. Not everyone could say the same.

"I think," she said carefully, "that in the interest of serving Cressmouth's entire community, the lending library should also be a resource for those whose grasp of English is not yet fluent. If we could offer instructional tomes, such as easy-to-read literature and the like, our shelves might become more accessible to everyone."

The solicitor tilted his head.

Meg hadn't mentioned Lucien's name, but in a village of this size, there could be little doubt she referred to one or more members of the le Duc family.

After a moment, Mr. Thompson gave a brisk nod. "I see your point, Miss Church. Our founder decreed Marlowe Castle for all of our neighbors, which means the lack you mention is indeed a grave oversight. I will see it is rectified immediately."

As the solicitor walked away, Meg's chest lightened. Even with the castle's resources, she wasn't certain how immediate the act of ordering books might truly be. A few days? Weeks? Hope fluttered within her. If the new books arrived before Lucien left... Perhaps better tools would help.

She turned back toward her picnic blanket just in time to see one of the children's runaway trundling hoops hurtle down the hill toward Jemima.

Meg raced forward to intercept the hoop and return it to the children. When she saw it was not the twins but rather Lucien le Duc hurrying to retrieve the errant hoop, she paused to wait for him in relative privacy next to the pine trees.

His steps slowed as well, as if he had doubts about the honor of her intentions.

She smiled wickedly. Smart man.

When he was an arm's width away, Lucien reached for the hoop.

She didn't let go.

He glared at her.

"Ooh, that's it, glower at me," she teased, batting her eyelashes. "Sulk for me. Mm, just like that. I *love* it. Do it again."

The corner of his lip quirked.

She still didn't let go of the hoop.

"Thank you," he said gruffly.

Grinning, she let him have the hoop. "Why don't you thank me with a kiss?"

His expression changed to comical horror.

"There are… *people* around us," he hissed.

"Well, if *that's* your only objection, then you know what I'm expecting next time." She gave him an exaggerated wink and fanned her chest, not entirely playacting.

Meg had expected him to scoff at her obvious teasing, not criticize her timing. This new development was very interesting indeed.

"You ruin… my best glares," he grumbled, and stalked off.

She watched him go before returning to the blanket and her cousin.

"You're dreadful to that poor man," Jemima scolded her. "He wouldn't have missed his trundle if he hadn't been watching you chase after Mr. Thompson."

"*Lucien* missed the trundle?" Meg perked up. "Perhaps he *wants* to be plundered."

"More likely, he hates the thought of anyone else plundering *you*." Jemima leaned back against the blanket. "I'm going to miss these picnics."

Meg lay down beside her. "Me, too."

Once the baby was old enough, there would be picnics again. But Meg knew what Jemima meant. They wouldn't be picnics like *these*, with talk of tumescent shafts and illicit liaisons. They would be too busy picking dandelions and chasing butterflies and counting swans in the lake. Wistfulness twisted within her. They would be absolutely marvelous picnics, but they wouldn't be the same.

Nothing would.

Just like the picnics, she would find a way to make her new circumstances different but marvelous, Meg told herself. She would secure a home of her own—somehow—and finally be able to stop running, changing, adapting, giving up. The next place would be permanent. She would finally put down *real* roots. Here in Cressmouth, with her community and her cousin and her new niece or nephew.

She turned her head toward Jemima. "Cruel of you to make me wait nine months to meet the baby."

"I shall do no such thing." Jemima's face glowed with contentment. "I'm three months along. The baby will be here before we know it."

Three months along. Meg's spine prickled. She did not have nine months left, but six. Perhaps less.

That was enough time to put down roots, wasn't it?

$\mathcal{L}$ucien paused just outside the threshold to the family smithy.

No, not the *family* smithy. It belonged to the Harpers now. Despite the same smells of leather and metal and grease, the same juxtaposition of intense heat from the forge and the bracing cold of the winter wind outside, the new owners' influence was everywhere. Not only was the smithy bedecked with boughs of holly, new faces laughed and shouted and frowned with concentration in every corner.

The smithy hadn't ground to a halt without Lucien. It was positively *bustling*.

For the first time since moving to Cressmouth, rather than pop inside to help out wherever he was needed, Lucien kept walking. Past the open doors, past the queue of waiting carriages, until he reached the street.

His heart beat uncomfortably fast. Not because he missed the smithy. He hated the smithy. But he'd loved being an intrinsic part, having responsibility, knowing he was productive, being important.

"*Pfft*," he scoffed beneath his breath.

Being a blacksmith hadn't made him important. It had made him *un*important. Fallen. Disgraced, if his parents had been alive to see it. He wouldn't be important until he got back to France, where the status quo had returned just as it had been before the revolution. His stomach tightened. If his parents were alive today, they wouldn't be dragged down the street and executed. They'd be fêted and fawned over, members once more of the glittering social sphere they'd wanted to share with their children.

If he wanted to be important, he just had to wait six more weeks.

He'd waited *this* long, hadn't he? Forty-seven-and-a-half more days was nothing. Which was why Lucien intended to spend as much of it as possible with the people he loved most: his family.

The door to his sister's house flung open

from within before Lucien even walked up the path. It was not the Skeffington butler standing at the threshold, but a pair of rambunctious ten-year-old twins.

"Uncle Lucien!" Annie and Frederick shouted as they tumbled out of the house to hug him.

Although they'd seen him mere days ago when they'd trundled hoops in the park, Frederick and Annie always greeted him with the same delighted exuberance. Lucien's chest tightened as he returned their embrace. Back in France, dignified *majordomes* might announce Lucien's name to throngs of aristocrats in elegant ballrooms, but part of him would always miss simple pleasures like these.

He ruffled the twins' hair. "Are your parents at home?"

The words came slowly, even though he'd rehearsed them in his head the entire walk over. If he managed to get the grammar right, his pronunciation never failed to cloud his meaning. But unlike many a tourist who had passed through the smithy, the twins had never made much of Lucien's limited command of English.

"They're in the cellar with Aunt Eve," Frederick said.

Annie tugged his elbow. "Do you want to make flower crowns? I picked harebells in the castle greenhouse."

"Or trundle hoops?" Frederick added hopefully. "Can you teach me a new trick?"

"After I speak... to your parents," Lucien promised them.

He did not need to ask directions to the cellar. Part of it had been converted into a small sitting room, and the rest provided storage to his brother-in-law Jack's vast collection of wine.

He reached the bottom of the stairs with the twins jostling behind him. At the clatter, Jack, Désirée, and Eve glanced up, startled, then broke into wide smiles.

"Perfect timing." Lucien's sister Désirée shot a teasing look toward her husband. "And to think we were debating whether to open another bottle of wine."

"I can think of no better cause for celebration than Lucien's presence," her husband Jack agreed. "Does anyone object to champagne?"

Lucien rolled his eyes in amusement.

Like his twins, Jack found himself in Lucien's presence on an almost daily basis. Although they were friends, what Jack really wanted was an excuse to enjoy Veuve Clicquot champagne.

It was a privilege to be the catalyst.

Lucien accepted a glass of bubbling champagne and took the chair across from his sister.

Annie and Frederick sat on the plush carpet at his feet.

Once the wine was poured, Jack made a face at Lucien. "We're trying to decide what to do with Eve's father."

Lucien turned toward Eve in surprise. "He is ill?"

"He's peevish," she corrected with a wry expression. "And bored. He thought retirement would make him happy, but now he has nothing to do. It's making him insufferable."

"We're discussing if having him join forces with Uncle Jasper would be a mistake or a solution," Désirée explained in French. "Bastien and Eve could take over her father's house, and Mr. Shelling could potter about the farm with Uncle Jasper."

The farm where *Lucien* lived? He stared at his sister in disbelief. Yes, Uncle Jasper could benefit from something else to do besides the occasional game of *vingt-et-un*, but Eve's father was not one of Lucien's favorite people.

He'd once opposed his daughter's courtship on the grounds that Bastien was *French*, which, if you asked Lucien, was the best trait of all. Perhaps the old man had finally outgrown his prejudices, but Lucien—

Had no say in the matter, he realized belatedly. This conversation was happening without him because the consequences would occur without him. He would be in France. They would be here. There was no reason to include him in plans about their future because he was not going to be a part of it. Rather than digging up weeds or making awkward small talk with Eve's impossible-to-please father, he'd be off waltzing with the *beau monde* in Paris, living the life he'd always wanted.

So why was his jaw clamped together and his stomach knotting in protest?

"Or perhaps the other way around," Désirée continued. "With Eve and Bastien at the farm, he'd be closer to the smithy, whilst Mr. Shelling and Uncle Jasper would have greater access to the castle and all its resources."

"I'm sure whatever the family decides will work out," Lucien said gruffly, and meant it. Come what may, the family always managed to do the best they could in any circumstance.

It was just the first time "the family" did not include *him*.

He was *glad* they were carrying on without him, if a little prematurely, he told himself firmly. It was a situation that would soon become the usual, and he did not want them to suffer in any way without him. He just hadn't expected them to find it so... easy.

From the moment of their parents' deaths, everything Lucien had done or planned or sacrificed, had been for the good of his family. Assuring a terrified ten-year-old and eight-year-old that everything was going to be fine, struggling every waking hour in a smithy he hated, forgoing his own chance at assimilation to provide for his siblings and then their ailing uncle... He would do it all over again, a thousand times if he had to, but the achievement Lucien had been most proud of was this chance to restore their heritage and give his siblings their home back.

And they weren't even interested.

Eve lifted her glass toward Jack. "This is excellent champagne."

"Don't salute me; salute *this* fellow." Jack grinned at Lucien. "In a few months, this lucky devil can bathe in buckets of the stuff if he has a mind to."

Eve feigned dismay. "Bathing in champagne sounds expensive. Never say Lucien is a *spendthrift*."

"Lucien is conservative to a fault," Désirée assured her. "He's more likely to cultivate his own vineyard than to depend upon anyone else's."

"A vineyard," Jack sighed dreamily.

"Be careful, *grand frère*," Désirée teased Lucien. "If Jack finds out there's so much as a single grape growing on your property, you'll never get rid of us."

Lucien gazed back at her, feeling two stone lighter. Perhaps that was the answer!

His family would never permanently abscond from England; that much was clear. But it didn't mean they couldn't spend extended visits in France, if Lucien provided an attractive enough incentive.

Living a life of leisure one day had been the dream that sustained him through year after year at the smithy. But a vineyard... who could object to that?

Their parents had owned one. If Lucien managed to get the family property restored, the old vineyard would be ready and waiting.

Because he'd grown up with it, Lucien was as familiar with grapes as he was with a lathe. It would give him renewed purpose and make his home an attractive family destination in one fell swoop.

"It's a deal," he told his sister in French. "If I provide the vineyard, you all must come and enjoy the harvest." His eyes fell on Annie and Frederick. "And learn French."

"We're learning already," Frederick answered in heavily accented French, without missing a beat.

Annie rested her elbow on Lucien's knee. *"Si nous apprenons le français pour vous, allez-vous apprendre l'anglais pour nous?"*

If we learn French for you, will you learn English for us?

Lucien stared at her in alarm.

He'd given up on English because he'd given up on England. He was leaving; who needed it?

But the answer was: his niece and nephew. His *family*. He wanted them to feel comfortable and fit in when they visited over there; they wanted the same for him whenever he was here. Honor and fairness meant he couldn't possibly put in less effort than a ten-year-old.

He'd sworn to protect his family. That included being a good uncle to Annie and Frederick, and any future nieces and nephews. What kind of uncle wouldn't even bother to try to communicate effectively in their language?

"*Je le farai*," he promised them in French, then corrected himself. "I will do it."

Désirée shot him a look of surprise. "You're studying the books I left you?"

Not exactly. Lucien cleared his throat rather than respond.

"I'm so relieved," she continued. "I was afraid that if I didn't have time to help, you'd give up entirely."

Lucien smiled blandly and hoped the heat rising up the back of his neck didn't lend its telltale flush to his face.

The truth was, staring at page after page of English text—whether in a children's book or the village Gazette—was not going to make him fluent. If he wanted to improve, he needed a tutor.

And if Désirée could no longer fill that role, he had no choice but to turn to...

Meg.

Lucien's face was definitely flushing. His entire body felt hot and out-of-kilter. He could only manage to keep Mademoiselle Church from his mind in brief snatches, and none of the images had anything to do with learning English.

Could he ask her? Making mistakes in front of another person was just as abhorrent to him as admitting when he needed help. It had worked with his sister because Lucien trusted her implicitly. He didn't know Meg well enough to determine if she was worthy of his trust. Yet something told him a woman as eccentric and fearless as she was, just might surprise him. Again.

The thought of *her* seeing his weaknesses made his palms clammy, but after everything else he had been forced to survive... He could do this, too.

Lucien set down his empty glass and rose to his feet. "Thank you for the champagne."

"Hoops later?" Frederick asked at once.

"And flowers?" Annie added.

"Later," Lucien promised. "There is something I... must do first."

Although he had never visited the Farrell residence—or paid a social call to anyone in this village—Lucien knew where to go. Cressmouth had only one dairy. Ten acres of farmland for grazing cattle; eight maids a-milking in the barn. That had to be the place.

His footsteps grew less sure the closer he drew to the front door, but he forced himself to rap the knocker anyway.

After a pause so long that he almost gave up the whole idea, the door swung open, revealing the exact person he'd come to see.

"Mademoiselle Church," he murmured.

"Meg," she corrected automatically.

Lucien ignored the strange jump in his stomach.

"Meg," he acknowledged. "May I come in?"

"May you..." She stepped aside at once. "Of course you can come *in*. You can come anywhere you like. I'd just been reading *Fanny Hill*—the climax, if you will—and for a moment I feared I'd conjured your image from the libidinous depths of my... Do you know what? None of that matters. Why are you here? Do you want some tea?"

What Lucien wanted was to be able to understand more than eighty percent of the things she said to him. Perhaps that was being generous. More than fifty percent? Surely that would be enough to prove to his niece and nephew how much they mattered to him, and that he was trying just as hard as they were.

"No tea." He took a deep breath. "I've changed my mind."

She frowned. "So you *do* want tea?"

"*No*. I want…" He clenched his hands. Why were these words such torture to say? "English lessons."

"English lessons." Her blue-gray eyes widened as though those two words were as foreign-sounding to her as they were to him. "From me?"

His cheeks heated. "You said…"

"Yes, of course I *said*, and yes, of course I will! Do you want to start at this very moment? I don't have any instructional materials with me, but I suppose we can begin with dialogue. That's how children learn, isn't it?" Her eyes widened. "Not that you're a child. You're *obviously* a man. A very big, very strong, very attractive—what I mean is, I don't think you have to stare at English to start understanding it. Maybe we should start with something simple."

"*Please* do something simple," he begged.

"Tell me if you understand these words." She stepped so close to him that her bodice nearly grazed his waistcoat. When she lifted her chin, her lush pink mouth was mere inches from his. She dropped her voice to a sultry murmur. "We're all alone. *Now* are you going to kiss me?"

His groin tightened. Yes, Lucien had thought about stealing kisses, blast it all. He had to physically restrain himself from reaching for her. He'd been thinking about kissing her ever since she put the idea into his head in the park. No, he'd been thinking about it for much longer than that. And here she was. Soft and eager. If he were to lower his mouth to hers, there was no one to witness him making a phenomenal, delectable mistake.

"You *do* understand," she breathed in wonder. Her face immediately fell. "And you're not going to do it, or else you'd have done so by now. Pity. Do let me know when you change your mind."

Lucien would definitely *not* let her know that he very much wanted to kiss her. If he let his guard down for even a moment, God only knew what might happen next.

"No lessons here." His voice was strangled.

Being alone with her not-entirely-teasing flirtations would not be conducive to concentrating on one's studies. The library wouldn't work; the castle was teeming with tourists and he did not want even one more person to witness him struggle. On the other hand... they clearly needed a chaperone.

"My house," he said firmly. "Tomorrow."

That would give him enough time to arrange for Uncle Jasper to be in plain view of the dining room table. His sister-in-law might even walk past a few dozen times if she wasn't working up at the castle. Maybe Lucien could even invite her extremely English father to move in six weeks early. They'd have to divide the bedchamber, which would definitely ensure Lucien got no designs on sharing it with someone else.

"Tomorrow," she agreed. "We'll start with an evaluation."

She meant evaluating his *English* proficiency, Lucien was sure of it. And yet, the way her gaze lingered on his mouth as though she was considering evaluating a few other things, right here and now...

"*À bientôt*," he blurted, and bolted out the door before he gave in to temptation.

CHAPTER 7

The next afternoon, Meg strode up to the smithy with a burlap sack in her arms and a few extra ringlets in her hair. She couldn't do much about her dowdy gown, but at least all but the bodice would be hidden by the table.

This was her first time on le Duc property. Meg's toes bounced in excitement. As she did not own a carriage or anything made out of metal, she'd never had a convincing excuse to visit the smithy until Eve had married Bastien. But now Meg no longer required a pretext! She was not only in possession of an utterly reasonable, perfectly *respectable* reason to pay a call, she'd been invited by none other than the man whose every brooding sulk made her toes curl and her stomach flutter.

Especially now that she knew all that dark glowering had been a shield to block others from glimpsing his vulnerabilities. His glares attacked first, "proving" he cared naught for others' opinions before they could have a chance to make them known. Meg imagined such an armored retreat to be a lonely place indeed. Her pulse quickened as she stepped from the road onto the private property line. There. Was she inside the shield yet? Her racing heart certainly thought so.

Meg picked her way between the clump of carriages awaiting service until she was standing at the threshold to the smithy. There was Lucien. Black boots. Tight-fitting buck-skins that outlined every muscle. Champagne-colored waistcoat. Black jacket. A slight curl to his brown hair. Strong jaw. Wide, delicious lips...

And no, she definitely was not yet behind his protective shield.

Not because the smithy now belonged to the Harpers. That might be what the title deed said, but the atmosphere inside the crowded workshop indicated the smithy still belonged to the le Ducs. Bastien and Lucien stood in the center, two bright suns about which everyone else merely orbited.

Although his brother was still talking, Lucien's dark brown eyes glanced over and his gaze met hers.

Meg felt it all the way to her toes. And heart. And nether regions. She was fairly certain even her prurient ivory mounds perked up at the sight of him.

Lucien murmured something to his brother, then strode up to greet her. He held out his hand for her bag.

She didn't hand it over.

He made an impatient gesture.

She enunciated clearly, "'Give me your bag, you daft woman.'"

He held out an aggrieved hand. "'Give me... your bag... you daft woman.'"

"No." She wrapped her arms tighter around the sack. "You didn't ask nicely."

His jaw fell open. "I... repeated..."

"What does 'daft' mean?" she inquired carefully.

He paled. "Er..."

"There, that was your first lesson. Never repeat a word if you don't know what it means." She swept past him. "To your cottage, I presume?"

Meg could feel Lucien's glare burning the back of her neck. She put an extra swing into her hips.

Just as they reached the cottage, thick pipes rattled on the side, followed by the loud gnashing and snorting of a large animal around the back.

"What," she asked politely, "was *that?*"

"Chef," Lucien answered. "We drop… rubbish into… his feeding trough."

Meg blinked. None of that could possibly be what Lucien meant to say.

She followed him into the house. "Your keep your chef in the rear garden?"

"Can't keep him in here," barked a gravelly voice from inside the drawing room. "Ever seen a hog root in a parlor? Can't say I recommend it."

Chef was a pig. A pet pig.

"Meg," Lucien said, pointing in her direction, then arcing his index finger toward an open door. "Uncle Jasper."

An older man with thinning white hair sat in a wingback chair between a dining table and a crackling fireplace, one leg propped atop a stool. The small table to one side contained a teapot and a deck of playing cards.

"I'd get up and bow if it weren't for this bloody gout." He craned his head toward Lucien and added in French, "Don't just stand

84

there, boy. Take the lady's bag and offer her a chair."

"He already grunted very gentlemanly for the bag," Meg assured him in French. "I was obstinate enough not to listen."

Lucien staggered backward as if thunderstruck. "*Tu parles français?*"

She shrugged. "Did you think only French people were clever enough to grasp two languages?"

He goggled at her in consternation. "Your... accent..."

"Oh, you expected a *bad* one. I can do that, too!" She straightened and affected a droll pose. "*Je appeler Meg. Je English. Je non intelligente.*"

"But... but..." he stammered in French. "You've been fluent *all this time?*"

"You never asked," she pointed out, this time without the bad accent. "Your uncle did say I could take a seat, didn't he? I'll have this one here. You sit across from me, and we'll start with—"

"Are you French?" he interrupted in desperation.

She let out a long sigh. "Yes. I am actually called 'Marguerite.'"

He brightened. "Really?"

"No," she said flatly. "But if you would have liked me better if I was, perhaps you ought to think about that."

Uncle Jasper hid a laugh behind a very unconvincing cough.

Lucien had the grace to flush. "But your French…"

"Ah, that." She began unpacking the contents of her bag. "I lived on the French Riviera for most of my childhood and moved around a bit after, but as soon as I could, I came back here."

His shock was comical. "You lived on the *Côte d'Azur* and came back *here?*"

She pushed a notebook in his direction. "I suppose that makes us both half-French."

A strangled sound escaped Lucien's throat.

The noise coming from Uncle Jasper's direction could only be described as chuckling. "Mind your words, young lady. Men have started wars for less."

"You were born in England?" Lucien demanded.

Meg nodded and handed him a pencil.

"To English parents?" he insisted.

She nodded again. "Mostly English. But I lived in France almost twice as long as you did. Surely that makes me just as French as you… and you, just as English as me."

He paled.

"Hope there's an apoplexy kit in that bag," Uncle Jasper warned.

"All right, I'll stop." Meg grinned at Lucien. "You're very, very French. The Frenchest Frenchman in all of Cressmouth. Possibly the whole world. And now this nice English-woman is going to teach you English."

"I don't know whether to kiss you or throttle you," he muttered.

"I have my preference, if we're putting it to a vote," she whispered back.

"Got a bad leg, not bad ears," Uncle Jasper called.

Meg grinned and pulled the tall stack of books out of her bag.

"I didn't know if you returned those others because you were finished with them or because you hated them," she explained. "So I brought a few of everything. I think the intended audience of a book is less important than whether its subject matter interests you." She fanned out the volumes until all titles were visible. "See anything that interests you?"

Lucien's dark gaze was not on the books, but on her. *"Beaucoup."*

Her cheeks heated and goosebumps of extra awareness danced on her skin.

"English only now," she said lightly, and picked one of the books blindly. "I brought a pocket watch. For every half hour of study in English, you earn a ten-minute break in French. Ready?"

He visibly collected himself, then swapped the history tome she'd randomly chosen for an illustrated guide to British fauna. *"Prêt."*

The half hour flew by surprisingly quickly. Lucien was an apt student, but Meg never lost sight of how private he was and how much of himself he was trusting her with by allowing this tutoring session to happen. Because he was willing to take such a personal risk with her, she was determined to treat these lessons with all the seriousness and respect he deserved.

When the minute hand marked the half hour, Lucien slumped back in his chair and rubbed his temples.

"Headache?" Meg asked with sympathy.

She remembered what it was like to move to France without speaking a word of the language. For a few months, there had been enough money for a governess. Afterward, Meg's education had been left up to... Meg.

"It gets easier," she told him in French.

His weary gaze met hers. "I know."

"Come on." She pushed to her feet. "Let's get some air. Why don't you introduce me to Chef?"

"He loves apples," Jasper called. "And boots, if you've an extra one in your bag."

Lucien shook his head fondly and held out his elbow. "This way."

Meg curled her fingers about his arm and felt his warmth all the way to her bones.

Rather than take her outside, he led her to a rear-facing window in the kitchen. A wooden pen stretched in a rough square just beyond the glass. Inside was an enormous black-and-white spotted pig.

"English people prefer dogs as pets," she whispered to Lucien.

His lips curved. "English people are boring."

"Not all English people," she protested in faux offense.

"Maybe not the ones who believe themselves half French," he conceded.

"The worst are the Frenchmen who refuse to consider themselves even a tiny bit English," she teased. "Eve told me you already purchased passage home. Why bother learning the language at this point?"

He looked surprised. "I'm not doing it for myself."

It was her turn to be confused. "Then who are you doing it for?"

"My family." He raked a hand through his hair. "Annie and Frederick are family now. With both my siblings married, who knows how many more nieces and nephews are on the way."

She feigned horror. "*English* nieces and nephews?"

"You don't get to choose who your family members are," he said gravely.

"Except when you do," Meg pointed out. "Désirée chose Jack, Bastien chose Eve, and your Uncle Jasper chose all of you."

His eyebrows shot up. "How did you know he wasn't an uncle by birth?"

"He's *English*." She tilted her head. "That's also how I knew you were part English, too. A true patriot would never claim an English as family."

"Where's my valise?" Lucien pretended to look under pots and pans. "I need to run away."

"You *are* running away," she reminded him. "You have a ticket to France."

"I'm not running *away*," he corrected. "I'm going *back*. Don't you ever think of it?"

"No," she answered honestly. "There's nothing there I want. What's over there for you?"

"My old life," he said without hesitation. "The one I would have had if I hadn't had to come here. It's too late to change the past, but there's still time to shape the future. I always thought I was doing it for my siblings' sake, but now that we're older, my priority has shifted to providing for my future children."

"So you *are* looking for a bride." Her chest fluttered. "What is your ideal woman like?"

He winced and averted his gaze.

"Let me help," she said flatly. "Not me."

It was a good thing she was a determined spinster, or his preemptive rejection might have stung.

"It's not... *not* you." He floundered. "It's just... I was raised to follow certain traditions—"

"I hate tradition," she informed him. "Rules are for ninnies."

"So when I marry—"

91

"I hate marriage," she added. "I'd rather be a spinster than a chattel."

"It will have to be someone of the same class I was born t—"

"You're an aristocrat?" She took a step back.

He made a face. "That depends how you define aristocrat."

He was. He *was*.

Lucien was from exactly the class of wealthy, indolent, have-everythings whose servants fed them strawberries and champagne while people like Meg sewed in cramped attics or breathed in black dust until their lungs stopped.

Her voice shook. "Do you have a title?"

"N-no."

"Are you in line for one?"

He hesitated. "Yes."

"Good God." Her throat went dry.

She tried to remind herself that he was still Lucien. That he hadn't created the primogeniture class system any more than she had singlehandedly caused the Revolution.

But if she was looking for a reason why they could never be together... she'd just found it.

He frowned. "Most women are... intrigued by the thought of a title."

"Intrigued isn't the word." She swallowed hard. "And I'm not most women."

Not that she could ever tell him why. If she was filled with distaste at the thought of the aristocracy, Lucien would be disgusted to find out her parents had fought on the side of the revolutionaries. They hadn't won, but they had fought.

And now both sets of parents were dead.

Bloody right, she wasn't going back. He could have France. She was finished with it.

*a*s little patience as she had for the flighty indifference of the aristocracy, Meg had to admit that Lucien was nothing like those lords and ladies.

At least, not while he was still here in England.

When they'd returned from their French break, Jasper was no longer in the drawing room. Nonetheless, Lucien had gone straight back to the books she'd selected for him and picked up his pencil. He wasn't learning English for himself, he had said. He was doing it for his family. For children who weren't even born yet.

It was difficult to keep a frosty demeanor in the company of a man like that.

This must have been what he was like as

an adolescent. The oldest of his siblings; put to work in a hot, grimy smithy of all places, after a life of luxury and coddling. She imagined he would have picked up each strange new tool without question, throwing himself wholeheartedly into any task, no matter how difficult or odious or painful, because it wasn't for him. It was for his family.

Lucien was many things, but he was not selfish. He was kindhearted and incredibly loyal. Everything he had ever done had been for someone else. Time and again, he consistently put others' needs first, even at the detriment to his own. Meg snuck another glance at him from beneath her lashes.

If the aristocracy had to exist… it could use more men like Lucien.

When the minute hand of the pocket watch reached the hour, he sagged forward and touched his forehead to the table.

"Ten-minute break?" he begged.

She took pity on him. "I think that's enough for one day, don't you? Why don't we work out a timetable. Did you want to do this once a week, twice a week…?"

"Every day, if you've the time." He added quickly, "I can pay you."

Her shoulders twitched. Meg could use the money, but she didn't want Lucien's.

"You can pay me in other ways," she suggested. "If your turgid member would like to visit my balmy feminine tunnel—"

He walked her to the door. "I am not making love to you for tutoring lessons."

"Who said anything about love?" She clasped a hand to her chest in faux shock. "You overstep yourself, sir."

"Do it!" Jasper shouted from the other side of the wall.

Lucien cast his gaze heavenward. "My uncle is a terrible chaperone."

"He really does have good ears," Meg said, impressed. "And great ideas. Here's another one: Don't answer yet. Tonight, when I'm not about, check with your swollen maypole in case there's a difference of opinion on how to proceed."

"I am not ruled by my baser instincts," Lucien said clearly.

She brightened. "So you admit your first instinct is in fact to surge forth like a great steed, plowing the tender field with a scythe of passion."

"That's nobody's instinct," he warned. "No one even knows what that means."

"Esteemed scribe Mr. John Cleland knows," she informed him primly. "He wrote an entire book about it."

"About—*wait*. That's what you're reading? The book you tried to give to me in the library is all about…"

"I *told* you it was more interesting than your books. Now you'll have to wait. I'm on the last chapter, and I can't wait to… finish."

Lucien closed his eyes.

"And when I say 'finish,'" she whispered, "I really mean—"

"Message received." His voice was hoarse. "The image of you with a book is now never leaving my mind."

She smiled earnestly. "The right literature is practically exercise."

He moaned again.

She stepped closer. "What was that?"

"It wasn't me," he muttered. "It was my turgid member."

"Oh, you two are going to have a *lovely* discussion tonight." She clapped her hands together.

He nodded as if in pain. "Many nights. You should go away. And stop talking to me in French. I understand all the words and it's battering my self-control."

"As you wish." Pleased, she turned toward the door.

He stopped her. "Aren't you forgetting something?"

She frowned. "What?"

"No witnesses."

Before she could quite take his meaning, Lucien took her face in his hands and lowered his mouth to hers.

This was what she had been missing. Any kiss she had ever felt before, any kiss she had ever seen or read about, vanished like steam from a kettle when compared to the heat of his kiss.

She pressed herself against him, heartbeat to heartbeat, close enough to feel his strength and to discern there was indeed a hot, sturdy maypole hoping to make her acquaintance.

Lucien was right. Theirs were not the sort of kisses one could hide in a public park. Theirs were the kind of kisses that must be stolen in secret moments, taken by force when the world conspired against them. She could not keep him, and he could not keep her, but nothing could stop their mouths from finding each other, again and again.

He tasted like the paradox he was; familiar and foreign, forbidden and irresistible. The more she tried to pull away, the tighter she clung to the hard muscle of his arms, the wide strength of his shoulders, the tousled softness of his hair.

When at last they pulled apart, neither had any breath left.

"There." The word scratched from Lucien's throat. "Now you know. No chemistry whatsoever."

"And now *you* know." She lifted her lips to his ear. "I'll be thinking of you tonight whilst you're thinking of me."

CHAPTER 9

*T*he following afternoon, Meg presented herself at the le Ducs' front step and lifted her hand to knock. The door swung open before her knuckles could graze the wood.

Lucien's tall, muscular frame not only filled the entire doorway, his domineering presence seemed to fill the entire village, erasing the rolling hills and the soaring castle and the endless evergreens until all that was left was Meg's pounding heart and the intense heat in Lucien's brown eyes.

"You missed me!" she said with delight.

He pulled her into his arms, slammed the door closed, and covered her mouth with his.

It wasn't a punishing kiss or a plundering kiss or any of the other fantasy kisses Meg had thought she wanted. It was a hundred times sweeter, a hundred times hotter, a hundred times *better*. And over far too quickly.

"I can't *stop* thinking about you," he grumbled when he finally broke the kiss.

"Just to clarify… you spent the night *thinking* about me, or 'thinking' about me?" She gave a suggestive wink.

He raised his brows blandly. "A gentleman never tells."

She lowered her voice to a whisper. "What if the lady *wants* to know every single sordid detail?"

He led her to the study table and pulled out a chair. "Then the lady will have to use her ample imagination, just like the gentleman did."

"Well, if the gentleman should ever tire of relying solely on his imagination…" She bit the end of her pencil and smiled.

"Trust me." He made a pained expression. "The gentleman is well aware that his imagination pales in comparison with reality."

"Especially when…" Meg pulled a small stack of books from her canvas sack. "Reality consists of reading comprehension practice, starting with the children's books you previously borrowed from the lending library."

He held up a hand in negation. "I didn't actually *read* them."

"You will today," she answered pertly, and handed him the first one. "Out loud, please."

After showering her with a series of impressively smiting glares, he sighed in resignation and opened the small volume to the first page. "Tom... Thumb?"

She nodded in encouragement. "Just so."

For the next hour, they made their way through the small pile, pausing after every page to discuss pronunciation and synonyms and metaphor.

When at last they reached the last page of the final volume, he shoved them all aside. "That's it. I will never pick up those books again. Not even to read to my children. I'll make up my own stories. *French* stories."

Probably Meg was meant to chastise him for his insistence in French's superiority over English, but the image of Lucien before a fire, reading aloud to an eager brood, had overwhelmed her with a strange sense of longing and emptiness.

His gaze met hers. "Do you want children?"

"No," she answered automatically.

It was true and not true. She didn't want

children with some handsome Town buck who would pass through Cressmouth for a fortnight and never be heard from again. That fear alone had spurred her to employ preventative measures like vinegar-soaked sponges that would prevent *Meg* from being the one to fill up her cousin's nursery.

And if some meaningless encounter had resulted in her being leg-shackled to some dandy she'd chosen for how he looked in evening dress, rather than anything he possessed between his ears? Meg repressed a shudder. Heaven help her. Nothing would be worse than losing her hard-won freedom, to becoming the property of a man, to being left at home, alone and forgotten, just as Meg's father had done to his own wife and child, even before he'd lost all their money.

No, thank you. That was not a risk she was willing to take for anyone, not even Lucien.

Not that he was asking. He was dreaming of the woman he *would* ask, once he returned to French high society, and the sort of debutantes an aristocrat deserved.

"I'll have at least two sons," he was saying. In French, of course. "And I hope that means I get to have a daughter or two along the way. I wouldn't be who I am today without my brother *and* my sister." His voice softened. "I want a big family for my children, too."

Meg did not respond. She had been an only child.

If there had been an heir for their fortune, such as it was, would her father have stayed home to raise his son? Or would that have spurred him to chase even wilder dreams, in the hope of creating an empire?

"Do you think about your future children often?" she asked.

"Every day," he answered without hesitation. "It gives me peace. Their generation will be able to enjoy the life my siblings and I were meant to have. Routs and ballrooms, tutors and university, wealth and comfort."

A world someone like Meg could not be less suited for. She had not needed the reminder, but perhaps it was good to confirm what she already knew. They would never have anything more than this.

Whatever it was that she and Lucien shared, it would end the moment he set sail for France.

CHAPTER 10

*L*ucien's pencil scratched across a fresh sheet of foolscap as he hunched over the dining room table, towering with stacks of books. In the week since he and Meg had begun daily lessons, everything had only become more challenging. The homework had gotten harder, limiting themselves to just the occasional stolen kiss had gotten harder...

What he was working on now were translations, to test his vocabulary. He was supposed to convert one page of an English children's book into French, and do his best to translate a page of Voltaire's *Candide* into English. He was now on his third page of each. Not because it was easy—translating was like trying to forge snowballs out of fire

—but because he wanted to please Meg. To impress her.

And to prove to himself that if he hadn't become a blacksmith, if the revolution had never happened and he'd attended the Sorbonne as his parents had planned, that he would have been every bit as worthy a pupil as his peers.

He glanced at the clock upon the mantel. His pulse jumped. Meg would arrive at any moment. He piled up his papers, tidied his appearance, and hurried out to the road to meet her.

As was the new usual, the drive leading to the smithy was clogged with carriages and tourists. Lucien was startled to realize he no longer missed being an essential part of the chaos. Instead of his world revolving about the smithy, it was starting to revolve around Meg.

Er, around *English lessons*. Student and teacher. That's all this was. Simple and uncomplicated.

Mostly.

His heart kicked harder at the sight of Meg nearing his drive. The simplicity of her plain brown pelisse and biscuit-colored gown made Meg's beauty stand out all the brighter.

Wild black curls that framed an expressive heart-shaped face. Bright blue-gray eyes. Plump, come-taste-me lips. Lucien shifted his stance. Although he could not greet her with a kiss, he had little doubt she could read his desire to do so in his gaze.

Before he could ask her how her day was going, a group of young ladies perched inside a completely impractical landau pointed his way and tittered.

He clenched his teeth together and turned his back to them.

Meg arched a brow. "Do you think they're talking about you?"

He sent her a flat look.

"Because I *know* they're talking about you," she continued. "You're not just Cressmouth's grumpiest blacksmith; you're the handsomest man in England."

His jaw tightened.

"Oh, did you want me to say 'France?' I cannot opine, because I haven't met all the men in France." She opened her eyes wide. "What if you're merely the *third* most attractive Frenchman?"

"Pardon my forwardness," one of the ladies called out. "Are you one of the twelve dukes of Christmas?"

"Allow me a moment to translate," Meg called back in English. She turned to Lucien and said in earnest French, "What you have just observed is the mating call of the wild Northumberland silver-feathered debutante. A migratory species, she can be found this far north in the winter only when her nostrils catch the scent of a nearby Eligible Gentleman."

"Tell her she and her giggling tourist friends can take their feathers and—"

"Alas," Meg shouted back to the tourists. "While this is indeed *a* le Duc, he is not the duke you're looking for." She gave a small wave. "Wishing you a pleasant day."

"Now what?" Lucien murmured, enjoying this more than he should.

"Now we flee," Meg whispered back. "Migratory Northumberland debutantes are wily creatures not to be discounted, especially when traveling in packs. They can occasionally be confused with well-chosen words, but only for a brief moment. Make haste, good sir, make haste!"

She looped her arm through his and assumed a runner's stance.

"The equally migratory southwestern French blacksmith," he informed her, "flees at a respectable, sedate pace, like a proper gentleman."

She wrinkled her nose. "That's not how anyone flees. That's how you get caught."

Was it? He tightened their interlinked arms.

Rather than head straight to the front door, they circled round toward the rear of the cottage. Chef's grunts and snorts grew louder as they approached. Meg's daily gift of apples had quickly made her a favorite.

"Someday, I'll bring you a boot," she promised Chef as she tossed him today's apple.

He grunted his appreciation as he made quick work of his treat.

She looked up at Lucien in apology. "I'm sorry there's no treat for you."

"I found one." Lucien's voice was husky as he brushed his lips against hers.

As much as he would have loved to kiss her thoroughly, the cottage's rear garden was too close to the busy smithy for comfort.

Not that the inside of the house afforded total privacy. The dining table where they held their lessons connected via an open doorway to the drawing room where Uncle

Jasper would be resting with his foot up and his eyes open.

Meg greeted Jasper as effusively as if he were her own uncle. The old man responded in kind, then held out his hand. Meg produced a stack of what appeared to be cinnamon and raisin biscuits and placed them in his palm.

Lucien stalked forward. "What is *that?*"

"Biscuits," Uncle Jasper answered, at the same time Meg said, "Bribery."

Jasper bit into a biscuit and sighed with happiness. "She's a good one. You should keep her."

Lucien's mouth fell open. "You bribed my uncle to matchmake?"

Meg sent Jasper a stern look.

"No," the old man said in English as he brushed crumbs from his chin. "She's paying me not to speak French to you anymore."

Lucien glared at them both. "Paying you. In biscuits."

"Reallocating existing resources, if it makes you feel better," Meg said in English. "Those biscuits came from the castle's reception hall."

"It does not make me feel better," he answered in French. "You don't understand. I can *express* myself in this language. Uncle Jasper is one of only a few people I can communicate eloquently with."

"Not anymore," Jasper said in English as he started in on a second biscuit. "She got to your siblings, too."

Lucien froze in horror.

"It's not a permanent embargo," Meg assured him in English. She patted his arm. "Your loved ones love *you*, and they've agreed to have the first hour of conversation in any given day take place in English. If you want to speak French, you absolutely can. But you'll have to soldier through an hour of English first."

"It'll take me that long to say anything at all," Lucien muttered in French.

"What's that?" Uncle Jasper raised a biscuit toward Meg in toast. "I'm an Englishman who only speaks English for the next fifty-five minutes."

Lucien glared at Meg. "There had better be biscuits in that bag for me."

"I have something even better for you." She bounced on her toes. "The castle solicitor has just informed me that the lending library has taken delivery of all four volumes of

Samuel Johnson's *Dictionary of the English Language!*"

He crossed his arms. "I would have preferred biscuits."

"I couldn't bring them with me," she continued, ignoring him, "not just because the set weighs over twenty pounds, but because Mr. Thompson correctly prefers such a valuable asset to remain in the library for safekeeping. He's arranged a quiet study nook for our tutoring sessions in the chamber next door. Where's your coat? I can't wait for you to see all the cunning little samples that help explain each word."

Intrigued despite himself, Lucien sent Uncle Jasper a final glower, scooped the study materials from the table, and escorted Meg out of the door.

"Mr. Thompson also procured a copy of Claudius Hollyband's *Dictionarie French and English*," she bubbled, "but it is horribly out of date and also cheating. If you wish to become fluent, you'll have to stop translating in your head and start thinking in the new language."

"*C'est—*"

"English, please," she sang out.

"*—difficult*," he finished.

"I know," Meg said softly. "I remember."

She curled her fingers about his arm and gave a comforting squeeze. "But you can do it. It's a matter of practice. One day you can't, and then the next day, the words are suddenly there, and you don't have to try to find them anymore."

"You swear... that will happen?" he asked doubtfully.

"I can't promise it will happen by Twelfth Night," she admitted, "but I assure you it *will* happen if you keep practicing English without using French as a crutch. If you don't know a word, ask me and I'll tell you. But during lessons, it's better practice to communicate in bad English than to mix English with French."

Lucien's entire body tensed. Part of him rebelled against the specter of becoming mute and awkward all over again with Meg, now that their long afternoons together had become the highlight of his day. On the other hand, he longed to be able to communicate effectively with everyone, to be eloquent with Meg in her own language, to read stories to his niece and nephew, to understand jokes and idioms and nuance.

"French... after?" he asked.

"French after," she agreed, and sent him an

impish grin. "French all night long, if you like."

He *would* like, very much, although that was not a liberty he intended to take. He could scarcely believe that less than a month ago, his opinions on both Meg and English had been very different.

Shame still burned at the memory of his initial flash of joy when she'd said her true name was Marguerite... and her admonishment to look inside himself to find out why.

Lucien didn't like what he'd found. It had made him question his own judgments, and wonder if he'd been discounting Meg for the same unfair reasons Bastien's father-in-law used to denigrate *him*.

It was not a nice revelation.

The truth was, Meg was extraordinary. Utterly fearless, as unstoppable as a tornado and with as heart big enough to crumble even Lucien's staunchest battlements. He might not comprehend why she would choose a wintry rural village over the southern coast of France, but he certainly understood why Cressmouth wouldn't be the same without Meg.

As soon as they reached the castle, she

raced up the stone steps with Lucien right behind her.

When they burst into the library, no one else was present, so she took him straight to the far wall, where all four dictionary volumes were displayed atop a long narrow bookshelf.

Meg flipped to the title page and read aloud. "A dictionary of the English Language: in which the words are deduced from their originals, and illustrated in their different significations by examples from the best writers, to which are prefixed a history of the language and an English grammar."

Lucien leaned forward, impressed. She was right to be pleased with the castle's purchase. The dictionary was incredibly thorough. So was Meg. He was starting to realize just how lucky he was not just to have her in his life, but also to have her as a tutor. She filled him with hope. No —more than hope. She filled him with *optimism*.

"Remember," she told him as they arranged themselves in the study nook. "Stop being so preoccupied about whether the words come out perfectly."

He could not hide his skepticism.

She smiled at him anyway. "Perfection

doesn't exist, and I wouldn't want it even if it did. The best way to miss out on everything that matters is to seek perfection instead of enjoying life."

Or perhaps, as Lucien was beginning to suspect, the realization that one's definition of perfection might evolve into something different than it once was.

"I've been working hard... on the translations," he said. "You assigned one page, but..."

He pushed the painstakingly copied pages in her direction.

Meg's face filled with horror.

Mortified, he tried to grab the pages back.

She held them tight.

"Your translations are lovely, but..." Her voice shook. "Why do men have such terrible handwriting?"

He flopped backward in his chair. "You are disappointed in... my handwriting?"

"I'm very sorry, Lucien." The sparkle in her eyes belied her grave expression. "The only man I've seen scribble even worse is Nottingvale. Don't sink to his level."

Don't sink to the level of... the wealthiest, handsomest, most high-ranking, most talked about and actual duke in the entire community?

"Wait." Lucien frowned. "When did you see Nottingvale's... penmanship?"

He was definitely not jealous. Penmanship wasn't a *euphemism*. There were all sorts of completely ordinary reasons why Meg would find herself in possession of one more document handwritten by the fashionable duke whose exclusive Christmastide house parties caused more furor than Wellington at Waterloo.

"When?" With a laugh, Meg rolled her eyes. "Only every winter. If the man wants any hope of his guests responding to his invitations, he needs to send them something they can read. I happen to have exceptional handwriting. I've kept a diary since a young age. I'll loan it to you if you'd like to glimpse my innermost thoughts on hollandaise or how my hair tangles every time I wash it."

Lucien doubted anything at all in Meg's diary would be appropriate for mixed company. He would most likely have learned English far quicker if he'd begun with that reading material rather than *A Very Pretty Pocket-Book*, but he still couldn't get past the image of Meg seated at a table just like this one, elbow-to-elbow with—

"Nottingvale has..." A man of business.

Several secretaries. An army of servants. A dowager. A *sister*. "He doesn't need…"

"Me?" she finished drolly.

Oh, very well. He *was* jealous. Unreasonably.

"Let me explain. You are an extremely competent blacksmith. *I* can do… *this*." She sharpened a quill at an odd angle, dipped it into the ink pot at the center of the table, and then began to draw fluid, curling lines on a fresh sheet of foolscap.

It said LUCIEN. Ostensibly. But each stroke was a calligraphic work of art; each curlicue as delicate as a spring leaf, each line a bold trunk from which a dozen other curls sprang forth.

He stared in awe.

She grinned at him unabashedly and whispered, "No one ever says no to one of these. My fingers are the discerning host's secret weapon."

He inclined his head. "You are… very talented."

"If only 'good penmanship' was a quality with which one could become rich," she said, then sighed. "Men get all the secretarial positions, and the planning of parties goes to wives. As soon as Nottingvale takes a bride, I won't even have seasonal invitations to amuse me."

Lucien leaned back. He suspected it was not amusement that Meg sought, but rather a longing to be needed, to be important. He knew what it was like to feel that way, and he knew what it was like for that comfort and certainty to go away.

Perhaps she performed this "favor" for Nottingvale for the same reason Lucien kept stopping by the smithy he no longer worked at, just in case someone was in need of a hand or good advice. He didn't envision himself as a lifelong blacksmith any more than Meg likely yearned to be the-spinster-who-addresses-other-people's-Christmas-invitations. But being part of something bigger than oneself was what made all the small stuff worth it.

"Would you *want* to be... a secretary?" Lucien asked. He supposed he could just as easily have said *a wife*, but voicing the word hadn't seemed easy at all.

She stared at the snow falling outside the window for a long moment before responding.

"I want to stay in Cressmouth," she said at last. "I've been living with my cousin, but they're starting a family, and I'm blocking the nursery. I've been hunting for a solution. Every afternoon as I walked to or from your farm, I took a different path in order to knock upon every door along the way and inquire whether anyone has a room to let."

The despondent expression on her face made the answer clear. "They do not?"

"They do not," she agreed in frustration. "It's no one's fault. Cressmouth is small, and so are the cottages. We don't have hotels and coaching inns. We have a castle."

He straightened.

"You're right," she agreed. "The castle has plenty of rooms. At a price per night greater than what I pay for a month's rent. Mr. Thompson offered me a discount of fifty percent, but even if I were willing to accept such charity, the price is still too dear."

She tried to smile.

"Besides, the last thing I want is to be a day-to-day renter like the tourists. I don't want something temporary. I want a home. A place I can hang portraits and make tea in my stockings if I want to. A place that will still be here ten, twenty, thirty years from now. Which means..." Her shoulders slumped. "I'm going to have to expand my search outside of Cressmouth."

He frowned. "How far outside Cressmouth?"

"Not more than a day's drive," she said without hesitation. "I'm about to be a... second cousin once removed? Let's say 'aunt.' Jemima and Allan are the only family I have left, and I hate the idea of even being that far away."

Lucien hated the idea of Meg being far away, too.

Somehow, when it was him doing the leaving, it hadn't seemed so threatening. So lonely. He'd been counting down the days to Epiphany because that was when he'd finally set sail for home... but what if he lost Meg even before that?

"What if there's... nothing?" he asked.

"There's something. Several somethings." She pulled a small stack of well-read letters from her bag. "Two rooms to let in Houville, three even further afield..."

Lucien's muscles tightened. He didn't want to touch those letters. The only thing he wanted in his hands was Meg. Without another word, he pulled her into his arms and kissed her.

This embrace was different from the countless stolen kisses after Meg had made some outrageous remark, or Lucien had managed to correctly conjugate the subjunctive tense. This kiss was not a reaction to something that had happened, but rather to all the somethings that would never happen. The afternoons they would no longer share with each other, the Christmases they would spend apart, a lifetime of separation yawning wider and wider in their future.

It was a kiss that said *remember me*, and *I'll never forget you*. That she did not have to try so hard to seem important because she already *was* important. To her family, to this village, to Lucien. He would never be able to hear an English accent without thinking of her. Hell, he'd never even be able to hear a *French* accent without thinking of hers, too. She would color everything that ever happened, even if she had to do it from afar.

Because this was also a kiss of goodbye. Of inevitability, of our-days-are-numbered. It was a kiss to burn into their memories because memories would soon be all they had.

Lucien knew what kind of life awaited him back home, just as Meg knew the kind of life she intended for herself. They could not be more different. Cultural differences might be a hurdle, but class differences were irreconcilable. They'd both seen it firsthand.

But even if they could surmount all those obstacles, he and Meg would soon have far more than a mere social chasm between them. They would be a sea apart.

This kiss was just another desperate attempt to hold onto something they both knew they could never have.

CHAPTER 11

*T*he more time Meg spent with Lucien, the harder it was to bear their time apart. What had begun as an hour or two of tutoring sessions had now become long, lazy afternoons that started around noon and lasted until well after sunset.

As the days grew shorter, so too dwindled what little time remained. Christmas was coming, and then Lucien would be going. There would be no more reason to come to this cozy little study nook. No reason to spread a blanket on the stone floor and place a basket full of food from the castle buffet in the center. No reason for romantic, post-tutoring indoor picnics beside the tower's big glass window, because there would be no Lucien to share any of it with.

You've known that from the beginning, she reminded herself as he refilled her cup of mulled wine. *Don't be greedy. You never expected to share private moments with him at all.*

But she *was* greedy. She *did* want more. And the things she wanted weren't things he could give her. She wanted him to stay here in Cressmouth, with her. She wanted to be more important than the French aristocracy. Meg of the Christmas Megs, scandalous spinster with no trace of a reputation and no path to riches. She wanted to matter anyway. She wanted to matter to *him*. She wanted to be enough.

As he handed her the warm mug, his knuckles brushed hers. The slight contact heated her more than the wine. She wanted more.

So did Lucien, because he cupped her face with his free hand and claimed her mouth with a soul-stealing kiss. It was everything she wanted and everything she feared. She *did* matter. He didn't tell her so in words, but with kisses like these, with longing glances, with the way he touched her hand or cheek or shoulder when he had no reason to, except for the same hungry yearning beating in her chest every time she looked at him.

She also knew she wasn't enough to keep him. How could she be, when perfect Cress-mouth wasn't enough, when the expanding families of his siblings and their new lives here weren't enough? She wasn't just Meg of the Christmas Megs. She was the Meg of this particular Christmas, and this Christmas only. Meg of November and December and five days of January.

And then she would be Meg of his past. Meg of his slowly fading memories. Meg the girl that he used to know.

None of which stopped her from matching every kiss with the same passion he showed her. If all they had was right now, she for one did not intend to squander a single moment of it. Fingers in her hair? Yes, please. Torrid kisses until they both gasped for breath? Absolutely. She wouldn't even mind using this blanket for reasons significantly less chaste than a picnic. She not only kept the door locked in hopes of impending debauch-ery, she even took the necessary precautions to ensure the only after-effect of lovemaking would be a great memory.

Instead, Lucien broke the kiss, slowly, the pad of his thumb caressing her cheek before he pulled away.

A tender smile softened his features before he turned toward the basket to put away what was left of their plates of cheese and bread and fruit.

Smiling. Her sulking, scowling, glaring, implacable Adonis wore an arrogant, self-satisfied smile because he'd been kissing *her*. Meg's heart skipped and her thoughts scattered.

Was it any wonder her chest felt like a thunderstorm raged inside, fierce and powerful, beautiful and dangerous? What they shared between them was all those things and more.

Lucien glanced out the window. "The sun is setting."

Meg nestled next to him. Sunset was her favorite time of day.

It used to be because twilight meant her cousin would come home from the dairy, and Meg wouldn't be lonely anymore. But Meg hadn't been lonely since she and Lucien began filling their days with each other. Now sunset was when study time ended, and having fun could begin.

Sometimes that meant talking. Sometimes that meant kissing. And sometimes that meant leaning against each other before a pink-and-orange stained sky, watching the occasional flutter of snowflakes drift down to the rolling evergreen fields below.

"Why is the snow always so beautiful?" Lucien murmured in English.

Meg tried to keep her grin on the inside. He'd been doing that more and more lately: accidentally continuing to speak in English for a short while, even after their study sessions concluded.

She didn't want to point it out and risk making him self-conscious—or horrified—but the diminishing pauses between words and the times when he spoke English without realizing it meant he was starting to *think* in another language, rather than the exhausting effort of translating in one's head.

Due to interactions with family friends and years of long hours in the smithy, Lucien's passive exposure to English had given him a large enough working vocabulary to understand meaning from context. But *recognizing* foreign words was one thing. Being able to recall and reproduce them at will was another thing entirely. A feat he conquered a little more every day.

Most of what remained was building the confidence to speak this new language with others.

"Everything is beautiful, when viewed from the top of a castle," she replied.

He raised his brows. "You are beautiful from any angle."

Before she could respond, he stole a quick kiss.

Had she thought this man difficult to please? Lucien was utterly, ridiculously, breathtakingly *easy* to please. He'd accepted Meg when she'd done nothing ladylike to deserve it. Found her beautiful despite a general appearance best described as *well suited for life on a farm*.

He loved his family wholeheartedly and unconditionally. Accepted his brother's English bride as a new sister. Welcomed his sister's new family as if they'd always been his niece and nephew, vied neck-and-neck for the title of Favorite Uncle. He even spoiled a fat pig as though it were a house pet, treating Chef like one of the family.

The person who had never been able to please Lucien was Lucien himself.

If only he could see how marvelous he already was. How wonderful he *always* had been.

"Look." He pointed through a far corner of the window. "We can see the dairy."

Meg's breath shook. *Seeing the dairy* was a daily occurrence she'd once taken for granted. Being forced to move yet again, even to the next village over, was going to be incredibly hard.

"I wish there was something I could do for Jemima." Meg twisted her hands with worry. Her cousin needed the nursery for her growing family, but Meg worried that the growing family would also need the money they would no longer receive once Meg wasn't there to pay rent. "There is so much to do to get ready for a baby."

"I don't know much about babies," Lucien admitted in French. "I suppose I should fathom it out before I start begetting heirs."

A teasing comment about being available to help practice the pleasurable acts of baby-making was on the tip of Meg's tongue, until the image of whom he'd beget his heirs *with* filled her mind.

Lucien did not only dream of returning to France. He dreamt of taking a French bride, making a houseful of French babies.

The reminder shouldn't make her feel so gutted. Lucien had always been open and clear about his aims, his motivations. Meg had known from the start that she wasn't what he was looking for. She was never what anyone was looking for. She was a good time whilst on holiday, before gentlemen returned to their real lives far away.

She hadn't even minded, until now. Being able to treat occasional liaisons with the same casual flippancy as any London rake had been one of the single greatest advantages of being a twenty-eight-year-old spinster with no reputation to protect. *She* could choose. *She* could chase. *She* could decide.

And then she could wave her fingers and say goodbye.

But this time, it wasn't so easy. She'd yearned to make a few naked memories in Lucien's strong arms from the moment they'd first crossed paths, but she'd never dreamed of *this*. Picnics in a castle tower. Long afternoons of baring their souls to each other under the guise of practicing a new language. Kisses that weren't a prelude to hurried intercourse in a strange bed, but a featured act in and of themselves.

She didn't want to wave goodbye to any of that. She wanted to hold tight and never let go.

But she knew it could never happen.

Their differences were more than him

wanting to be Parisian *haut ton* and her aspiring to stay right here in a rural village. More than him wanting a new life and her wishing she could keep hers just as it was.

Even if none of that were true, and Meg actually wished to be some man's wife, Lucien believed in the same stark class disparity that people like her parents had started a revolution against. Lucien believed he *deserved* the best comforts in life due to the happenstance of his bloodline. The same happenstance that meant people like Meg and her family did *not* deserve ballrooms and education and comfort.

As unjust and distasteful as she found such views, Lucien would be appalled to learn just how far her family had gone in their quest to disrupt the status quo. Her father had risked every penny on investments he hoped would provide a better life for his family, but the coal mine had been a last resort. Before that, he'd been out in the streets, protesting shoulder-to-shoulder with other fathers who could never rise through the ranks because there *were* no ranks at the bottom.

Aristocrats like Lucien's parents were the reason farmers like Meg's family could never win a better life.

And desperate rebels like Meg's father were the reason Lucien had lost his parents.

His family might not have chosen to be born with the blue-blooded advantages of High Society, but men like Meg's father had enthusiastically chosen to tear the nobility's advantages to shreds by any means and at any cost.

Lucien would never forgive her if he found out.

CHAPTER 12

*S*unday was Lucien's favorite day to be inside the smithy.

It was the one day of the week when it was closed; when there was no obligation for anyone to be inside of it at all. No demanding customers, no confused apprentices, just Lucien working on this or that for the sheer fun of it.

Granted, the only reason it was fun at all was because he was doing it for Meg.

Not that she knew he was voluntarily spending time in the smithy, or what he was doing it for. The reason—like so many reasons these past two months—was her. She was his first thought every morning and his last thought every night. She was the reason that, after nineteen years dreaming of the day he would finally leave England, a tiny part of him didn't want to go.

No, that wasn't quite true. *All* of him wanted to go. None of him wanted to leave *her*.

There was no sense hoping she'd come with him. The thought of moving a few miles away was enough to put her into a panic. She loved Cressmouth. And she was English. She would no more abandon her motherland than he intended to give up his. He knew what it was like to resent the very world around him. He liked Meg too much to ever want her to feel that way about him.

A shadow fell into the open doorway, and Lucien glanced up to see Wilson, the man who handled the local post. Although Lucien recognized him, Wilson was not a frequent face at the le Duc farm. Until recently, the entire family lived under one roof. Even now, if Lucien's brother-in-law wished to send a message, he'd dispatch one of his footmen to deliver it. Wilson only tended to appear when his carriage required servicing.

Today, he was on foot, a letter outstretched in one gloved hand.

"Good morning," he said cheerfully. "An item came for you."

Lucien accepted the letter with his usual noncommittal grunt, then remembered he was now proficient enough to at least handle a transaction like this with some semblance of grace.

"Thank you," he forced himself to mutter in English. "It must be cold out."

Wilson stared at Lucien as though he'd grown carriage wheels for horns.

The back of Lucien's neck heated. What had he bollocksed? The grammar? The pronunciation? The—

"Downright balmy," Wilson said, his usual laugh lines returning. "The sun's not hot enough to melt the snow, but it makes for a splendid day outside. I've no doubt every child in Cressmouth is currently running amok in the castle park."

Lucien inclined his head. "Thank you for the warning."

Wilson grinned at him, tipped his hat, and continued on his way.

Lucien's heartbeat sped as a sense of victory flooded him. A dozen words at best, and he'd nearly sent the postman into a dead faint in the process, but he'd done it: Lucien had just had his first solo conversation in English with someone who wasn't his family.

Or Meg. Who sometimes felt like part of his family. He couldn't wait to tell her.

That was, to tell her about the conversation in English. Not the way she jumbled up all his feelings inside.

He pulled off his leather gloves and broke the seal to the letter. If he'd thought its contents might return his galloping heart to a more sedate pace, he was sorely mistaken. *This was it.* The letter he'd been waiting for!

Lucien's hands shook as he read its contents a second and a third time. Thanks to his distant relation to the *duc d'Orléans*, who had become king in the wake of Napoleon's defeat, Lucien's petition had been answered.

The court had provided a date in February to hear him speak, and would then rule on the possibility of returning the le Ducs' lost familial lands, thereby restoring their rightful place in French society.

Elation buoyed him. It was finally happening. The family home, the old vineyard, everything they'd lost in the revolution would belong to the le Ducs again.

Well, everything except their parents. Some things, once lost, were gone forever. But Lucien had fought his hardest to regain everything that *could* be won.

His siblings might not plan to return now, but this gave them options for the future. It gave their *children* options, and so on for generations. It was Lucien's duty to see this through, to provide the very best for his family.

He looked at the date again. The first of February. That was more than enough time to set sail the sixth of January as planned, and travel straight to see the king. Lucien hoped the vineyard was still in working condition, and that his childhood home was not in need of too many repairs. The sale of the smithy had paid handsomely, but Lucien still needed to live off that money for the foreseeable future. Once the house was livable and the vineyard profitable, he would never need to worry about poverty or having a roof over his head ever again. His life would be—

Almost perfect.

He swallowed hard. The beginning of his sparkling new life meant the end of his current one, here with Meg. His chest tightened. He folded the letter carefully and slid it into his waistcoat pocket next to the tickets home that he never let out of his reach.

It was morning still. Far too early for afternoon lessons. But with confirmation that everything he'd worked for was finally coming true, the one thing he desired most was not to waste a single moment that remained.

Which meant he was done with the smithy.

Lucien was going straight to Meg.

He hung up his leather apron, donned his winter outerwear, and retrieved a parcel before readying the phaeton.

When his brother had first painted the carriage with French flags, Lucien had not been amused. He was as patriotic as any Frenchman, but they hadn't had money to waste on nonsense. Red, white, and blue paint was just as unnecessary as the dandified frippery Sébastien insisted on clothing himself in, whenever he wasn't in the smithy.

But his *petit frère* hadn't meant any harm. He'd been doing something Lucien had long denied himself: attempting to enjoy the life they had *now*, rather than devote all his energy to an unknowable future.

Lucien lifted the reins. He *did* know the future. It was there in his waistcoat pocket. The ship would sail the sixth of January. The audience with the court was the first of February. In the meantime, he could finally enjoy the *present* guilt-free. And all he wanted was Meg.

He turned his horses toward the dairy just in time to see Meg and her cousin returning from a stroll.

Lucien pulled alongside them. "Fancy a drive?"

Jemima merely shook her head, as if the sight of taciturn Lucien le Duc speaking English and soliciting rides like a hackney driver wasn't unusual in the least. "Not this time. You two go ahead."

Meg arched a brow. "I see you've decorated the carriage."

He held out a hand to help her up.

"Is it too subtle?" he whispered. "I'm thinking of adding '*WE ARE FRENCH*' beneath each flag in large letters."

"But would you write it in French or English?" she countered. "A true Frenchman would write in French, but if you do so... your intended audience won't be able to read it."

"Existential crisis." He clutched his chest. "I will need to ponder long and deep about this."

She fanned her bosom. "I *love* things that are long and deep."

He tried to send her a quelling glare. "Be careful what you wish for."

Her eyes sparkled. "Because I might get it?" She folded her hands together and assumed a pious expression. "Dear heavens above, in the name of all that is bosomy and heaving, if you could grant my sultry cavern of moist pleasures the opportunity to personally welcome Lucien's engorged maypole of sinful delights—"

He burst out laughing. "Am I to understand you finally reached the climax of your book?"

"Many, many times," she assured him. "I can read it to you later, if you like. Just the good parts."

He slid her a suspicious glance. "What percentage of the book contains 'good parts?'"

"All of it," she replied earnestly. "I hope you're prepared for many, many long nights exploring the torrid depths of quality literature."

His body tightened at the possibility. "How are you not married?"

She blinked. "I don't know how much of our current conversation you were unconscious for, but most gentlemen frown at ladies in search of a fine maypole."

He shook his head. "They might not relish the thought of you sampling *other* maypoles, but any husband with a pulse would want a wife who enjoyed their bed. *I* certainly want—"

A bride like you.

Lucien clamped his teeth together before the words could spill out. Where had that thought come from? He'd known since he was small what sort of wife he was expected to take, and it certainly did not match Meg in any way.

And yet...

"Most gentlemen," she said with a laugh, "fail to consider that not all women wish to *be* brides."

"Most women," he pointed out, "have few options beyond 'marrying well.' What is a spinster supposed to do for the rest of her life?"

She arched a knowing brow.

He closed his eyes. "Please don't say 'sample maypoles.'"

She pantomimed sewing her lips closed.

"That is not a life plan," he chided her. "One day, you're going to be—"

"Too exhausted to... *erect* another maypole?" She fluttered her lashes. "When that

day comes, I'll take up knitting. Or horti-
culture."

"Or letter-writing?" He slid her a look.
"Rumor has it, you have excellent
penmanship."

"Those gossips!" She let out a dramatic
sigh. "Every word is true."

He pointed at a large package near her
feet. "That's for you."

Her bravado faltered. "For me?"

"Open it."

He kept his hands on the reins and his eyes
on the road. The gift was nothing. It couldn't
be anything. Lucien was not in a position to
make promises about things he already knew
would not happen. But he was the type of
person who tried to shape the future as best
he could.

Meg untied the knot and peeled back the
brown paper.

"It's a *slope*," she breathed. She stripped the
paper from the portable desk, and lifted the
flat writing surface in order to peer inside.
"Stocked with paper, pencils, quills, and ink."
She looked over at Lucien, a question in her
eyes.

"Just because we're in separate countries,"
he mumbled, "doesn't mean I want to stop

146

bickering with you."

She grinned at him. "I never bicker. I'll send you long letters, filled with my innermost thoughts about maypoles."

"Please do not."

"What if I just keep you apprised on the current situation with my bosoms?"

He could not prevent an involuntary glance in their direction. "I…"

"Ooh, that wasn't a 'no,'" she said with an approving nod. "Bosoms it is. I'll include illustrations."

His throat went dry.

"I can imagine very well," he managed, before realizing his rebuke was tantamount to confessing how much time he spent imagining all the ways he longed to interact with her bosom and every other part of her.

"Thank you for the gift," she said softly. Her expression was one he could not decipher. "I'll miss you, too. I'd kiss you if we weren't in public."

Lucien was already steering his horses toward the private lane that cut through the evergreens.

"I received news from the court," he said suddenly. He'd meant to save the announcement for his siblings, yet his first impulse had been to come find Meg.

"About your petition?" She pulled back. "Are you an aristocrat again?"

"Almost." His words tumbled out on top of each other. "I know I mustn't sell the bear until I've slain it, but others have had their rights restored, and our family has a direct line to the Crown. I expect our holdings to be returned in February."

"Congratulations." Meg's voice was oddly hollow.

Frowning, Lucien glanced in her direction.

"I'm glad about your family home," she said quickly. "I'm sorry you lost so much. I just…" Her voice dropped almost too low to hear. "…wish you weren't an aristocrat."

He touched her arm. "I don't have a title."

She rolled her eyes. "You're in line to one, and we both know that's good enough for the *beau monde*."

"It's not good enough for you?"

"I don't need titles at all. I'm not impressed with people who were born 'important.'" Her gaze was piercing. "Don't you want to be important because *you* are?"

"There's nothing wrong with being 'born'

important," he protested.

"Isn't there?" she muttered.

Now that they were alone among the hills of evergreens, Lucien pulled the horses to a stop. "You don't understand."

"Maybe it's you who doesn't understand." Her eyes flashed. "Returning to France won't bring your parents back. The past happened. It's done. Isn't it time to think about the future?"

"The future is *all* I ever think about." His voice shook with emotion. "I promised my parents I'd take care of my siblings and give them the life they were meant to have."

She lifted her chin. "Maybe they *are* living the lives they were meant to have."

"Maybe *you* are," he said, "and maybe you're not. You like being a spinster because it gives you freedom. It gives you choices. Why wouldn't I want that for my own family? If it's in my power to give my children the opportunities they deserve, I would give my life to do so."

"That's exactly what my father always said," she mumbled. "It didn't work."

"I will make it work," Lucien said fiercely. "I owe it to past and future generations. The day my parents were killed, we had gone to market. Bastien and Désirée were at home in the nursery, but I was grown up. Fifteen was practically a man. I would have done anything for them. When I saw them being dragged away, my only choices were to run away or stay and fight."

"What did you do?"

"Ran away." His voice was bleak. "I never forgave myself. Even though I ran at their request, ran so I would not be taken too, ran to protect my little brother and baby sister. Together, we ran all the way here." He tightened his fists. "I'm tired of running. I'm ready to fight for what was ours to begin with."

"Maybe you're not ready," Meg said. "Maybe you're running away again. Maybe England scares you and Cressmouth scares you and *I* scare you, and the easiest thing to do is hop on a boat and leave."

Anger seared through Lucien's veins.

"There hasn't been one easy day since the night my parents died," he snapped. "There's a difference between running *from* and running *to*. Home is never the wrong place. If you think it's easy to walk away from my family… If you think it's easy to walk away from—"

You.

"Around here," she said quietly, "you already *are* a member of the aristocracy. You don't just live in Cressmouth; you're part of it. Our legend of the twelve dukes of Christmas wouldn't be true without you."

He shook his head in denial. "It has nothing to do with me. And I can't stay."

"Neither can I," she said with a frustrated sigh. "I found a room to let. In Houville."

His heart jumped. "Houville?"

She nodded. "I won't be here to miss you when you're gone. I've written to ask if they can reserve it for me for a month, because I'd like to help Jemima set up the nursery before I leave. But if they cannot, I will take the lodging now." Her smile did not reach her eyes. "I cannot risk having nowhere to go."

He frowned. "Your cousin—"

"—would never throw me into the street. You're right. There's not a sweeter soul in all of Cressmouth. That is why I would never knowingly inconvenience her. Jemima has done so much for me. The least I can do is leave when she asks."

His chest hollowed. "But Houville…"

Isn't Cressmouth.

Even if he came back from France one day to visit family, Meg wouldn't be here. Cress-

151

mouth wouldn't feel like Christmas at all. It would feel empty. Lonely.

But she was here right now, and so was he.

He took her face in his hands and kissed her as if the fire between them could banish the winter forever. As if all he had to do was close his eyes, and the distance between two countries would disappear.

As though if he kissed her long enough, hard enough, deep enough, his kiss would carve an indelible hole in her heart that only he could fill, just as she had done to him.

But when they lifted their heads, snow was falling as though to spite him. It was still winter.

And time to say goodbye.

CHAPTER 13

*L*ucien was just stepping out of the smithy when a carriage pulled to a halt in front of him. Meg's cousin Jemima and her husband Allan were inside.

Jemima held out a small folded square of parchment. "Message for you, sir."

Lucien narrowed his eyes. "You drove over here to deliver a note from Meg?"

Jemima shook her head. "We're visiting Allan's parents for the week, while I can still travel."

"Then I won't keep you." Lucien stepped back. "Enjoy your visit."

As soon as their carriage was out of sight, he unfolded the tiny missive. It bore just four words:

Home alone.
<u>*Come*</u> *over.*

He shook his head fondly. Meg was impossible. And Lucien was definitely coming over.

When he arrived, he half-expected her to greet him at the door wearing little more than stockings and garters.

Meg not only opened the door fully clothed, she had three iron nails protruding from one corner of her mouth and a hammer in her hand.

"*Dieu merci.*" She shoved the hammer to his chest and dropped the nails into his palm. "Come tell me if this shelf is crooked. I feel like it's crooked. No one ever told me putting up shelves was so *difficult.*"

He trailed her into the cottage. "Your cousin left an hour ago, and you're already remodeling her house?"

"Not the house." She motioned him to follow her. "The nursery. They've been picking up things they need for the baby, and stacking them in a corner of the drawing room. I want it to be ready for them when they come back."

His heart skipped. "You're moving to Houville next week?"

"I have to start paying rent next week, if I want the room." She shrugged. "I might as well give Jemima and Allan the last few months of privacy they're ever going to have."

"But next week is Christmas," Lucien stammered. "You can't leave before Christmas. Maybe your cousins don't want you to go."

"They literally asked me to go," she reminded him. "They need the nursery."

"They don't need it next week," he insisted. "And it's not like they'll *never* have privacy again. The baby will eventually…"

"Turn twenty-five and marry?" Meg finished with a droll expression. "Excellent point. I'll be sure to explain to them that although I *could* have given them privacy, I chose not to because they'll have a second chance for it after a quarter of a century. Provided the baby doesn't become a spinster."

Lucien glowered at her. What he meant was that *he* didn't want to her leave, and she knew it.

She gazed back at him blandly.

He ground his teeth. She was going to make him say it.

"I—"

"You're leaving a fortnight later. I know." She pointed at the wall. "Can you straighten that shelf before you go?"

He tossed the hammer onto the bed, then realized it was likely *The* Bed; the one in which Meg indulged her most wanton literary fantasies. He turned to a side table. There it was. *Fanny Hill.* He could be wrong, but from this angle it looked like every single page had been dog-eared.

"I'll read to you later," Meg promised. "Tell me your favorite *fantaisie*, and I wager I can turn to the right page on the first try."

Lucien didn't need to read a book in order to find his favorite fantasy. He was staring right at her.

"You're right." She moved the hammer from the bed to the table and trailed her fingers over the mattress. "We have all week to put up shelves. Why not start with dessert first?"

With a single step, he closed the space between them. She was in his arms, returning his kisses, and then they were falling backward, caught by the softness of the mattress and the warmth of each other's embrace.

What happened to his cravat? Somehow it had been tossed to the floor. Just like his jacket, his waistcoat. It was hard to pay attention to his rapidly disappearing clothes when his lips were busy kissing Meg's, and his hands were occupied with loosening the back of her gown.

When she straddled him to lift his shirt over his head, he took advantage of the opportune position to taste her breasts. She gripped his hair with her fingers and rubbed herself against him as he teased and licked. He could do this forever. He could do *anything* forever, as long as he was with her.

He was in love.

Lucien stopped licking.

Meg glanced down. "What's wrong?"

"*Mon Dieu.*" He closed his eyes.

She lowered her hand to cup his cheek. "What is it?"

Love. So, what was he going to do about it? The wise thing would be nothing. The reckless thing…

He flipped her over so that her back was to the blanket and Lucien was on top. It did not make him feel like he had the upper hand. He was just as lost as ever. The only thing he wanted was her.

"Marry me," he said before he lost his nerve.

Her eyes widened. "What?"

She didn't need him. He understood that. She had no desire to wed. He mostly understood that. But if she wanted *him* enough...

"Marry me," he repeated.

She bit her lip. "No."

He stared at her. "You don't want to?"

"*You* don't want to," she corrected.

"I *do* want to. That's why I asked you."

"You desire me." She brushed her fingers to his face. "It's not the same thing. There are too many reasons why it wouldn't work. But I desire you, too. And here you are, in my bed. I know what *I'd* like to do next. What do *you* desire?"

He gazed down at her. He'd never expected to fall in love, never expected to want her to marry him, never expected to ask twice and be rejected soundly in the space of a minute.

Now that he knew any lovemaking would only be temporary, now that he knew for certain they had no future, what was he to do? Put up a shelf and run home? Or stay in the place he really wanted to be, if only for the night?

CHAPTER 14

*M*eg held her breath.

She hated to hurt Lucien—if, indeed, the fog of passion had briefly convinced him he truly wished to marry her—but she knew better than anyone that she wasn't what he wanted. At best, she was merely something he desired.

Nonetheless, men did not take kindly to rejection of any type. Even if he well knew that he hadn't *really* wanted to marry her, being told 'no' was a bucket of frigid water. She would not blame Lucien for walking away.

But he did not.

He brushed his thumb across her lower lip and followed it with a kiss so sweet and pure, she felt it to her toes. He wasn't leaving. He also wasn't rushing. Instead of resuming the frenetic speed in which they'd half undressed each other, he seemed to be taking his time. Drawing each moment out as if this was the first and last time they would ever find themselves sharing a bed.

That's what it was, she realized, the truth sharp and bittersweet. A night of goodbye.

Knowing this was the only time she would ever have him made her senses all the more sensitive, as though her mind was desperately cataloguing every detail in order to recreate this moment in her memory again and again.

The gentleness of his hands and the passion of his kisses. The slight scratch of his unshaven jaw against the side of her breast. The scent of his skin: soap, leather, sandalwood. The erotic feel of his breath and his tongue against her bared flesh. The heat in his gaze as he paused to make certain he was giving her everything she wanted.

Against her breast. "Here?"

Yes.

With her nipple. "Like this?"

Yes.

Between her legs. "Harder?"

Yes, yes, yes.

She had never said yes so many times and so breathlessly in her life.

No one had ever *cared* if they were touching her how she wanted to be touched, kissing her how she wanted to be kissed, penetrating her as she wanted to be penetrated. She hadn't known that hearing the question, that forcing herself to respond out loud would be just as arousing as the act itself.

Slower. Harder. Pinch. Suckle.

Kiss me. Grab me. Deeper. Faster.

Words she'd never said aloud. Words she only thought, only dreamed of, only longed for. She wrapped her legs tight about him and tried to give him everything that he was giving her.

"Do you like it this way?" she asked, surprised at the shyness in her voice.

She could feel his buttocks tighten.

"I've been turgid since the day I met you," he growled.

She grinned at him. Grinned, during lovemaking. This wasn't a physical release between strangers. He knew her better than any man ever had. He was right here with her. Meeting her eyes. Filling her soul. Making love to *her*. To Meg, because he desired her. Understood her. *Chose* her.

He reached between them. "Do you want me to touch you here?"

Yes. Please, yes.

"Meg?"

She met his gaze. Stared right into his eyes as she boldly said, "*Yes*. If you touch me there, I think I'll…"

He touched her there.

She shattered around him. Had been halfway there just from hearing him ask the question. From hearing herself say *Yes, I want it* as his shaft stroked deep within her. Was brought to her peak yet again when she felt him reach his own.

Had she thought she'd found pleasure before? She was spoiled now for all other men. Didn't even want to *meet* any other men. No one would ever hold a candle to Lucien. Was it any wonder she'd fallen in love with him?

Her heart hiccupped. Not because she was surprised she'd fallen—anyone would have— but because she was only now realizing how utterly destroyed she would be when he left. She held on as tight as she could.

He let her, for a while. Held her just as close and just as tight. And then he kissed her forehead and reached for his clothes.

She let him go. Watched in silence as he

pulled on his breeches, his shirt, his waistcoat, his jacket. Watched him tie his cravat before picking up the hammer and straightening the crooked shelf, just like she'd asked him to do.

And then he reached for the door.

"I meant it." His voice was quiet, but clear. "When I asked you to marry me. I won't bother you again. I'm sorry we aren't a good match, but I am glad my first time was with you."

She bolted out of bed, naked. "*What?*"

But he was already gone. She could hear his footsteps, fading. The sound of the front door.

The endless emptiness of goodbye.

CHAPTER 15

*M*eg fell backward onto her bed and stared unseeingly at the ceiling.

She, who had sworn never to want the same man twice, wanted Lucien forever and ever.

He, who had sworn never to settle for less than fellow French nobility, had proposed to *her*. And *meant* it.

Aargh, how she had longed to say yes! To believe she *could* say yes would turn her entire world upside down. Life had shown her, again and again, that nothing good ever lasted, and the same was true now. Yes, he'd walked away because she had said no. But if she hadn't... Lucien would have *run* away.

She wasn't just some unimportant English farm girl. She was the granddaughter of unimportant *French* farmers. Lucien's parents might have hoped the rebellion would die down, but Meg's parents had actively fought in the revolution. They were the exact sort of people whom Lucien rightfully blamed for murdering his parents. She could not hide a secret that big. Not from someone who trusted her enough to want to marry her. And the moment Lucien found out the truth...

He'd be gone.

Which left what? She gathered clumps of blanket in her fists and sucked in a shaky breath. Houville, that was what. Moving to a slightly larger village full of complete strangers and cheap rooms to let, because that was all she could afford to do.

Living alone, as appeared to be her destiny. Too far to walk to see her cousin. Too far to even see the castle. A thousand miles away from France and Lucien.

Meg rubbed her face with her hands and turned onto her side. The pillow smelled of Lucien. She hugged it to her chest and refused to cry, no matter how sharp her eyes might sting. She would not let her tears wash away any trace of him.

She *did* want him. More than anything. He was smart and sweet, family-oriented and loyal, and best of all... he wanted *her*.

She'd always thought that taking a husband meant losing her freedom, losing autonomy, losing any semblance of control over her own life. But now that she'd turned down Lucien's offer, it was saying *no* that had sent her on a spiral of loneliness. She didn't feel stronger without him. She felt empty.

So what was she going to do about it?

Meg pushed herself upright and stared at her simple muslin gown laying crumpled on the floor.

Even if she were an aristocrat too, she would still be scared to give up everything she knew and the roots she'd desperately been trying to put down, just to gamble on an unknown. Saying yes to Lucien meant saying yes to leaving Cressmouth, to leaving her cousin, to leaving England. It meant saying yes to a different country and a different world than the one she was used to.

But her biggest fear, her secret fear, wasn't having to begin again with strangers somewhere new. She was terrified of starting a new chapter with someone she *knew*, someone she hoped to *keep*, creating a home together in which she hoped to *stay*. Leaving of her own free will was so much more palatable than being rejected.

It was also more cowardly.

Hadn't she accused Lucien of running away from Cressmouth rather than giving it a chance? What was she doing, if not the very same thing?

With trembling hands, Meg snatched up her gown from the floor and pulled it on.

She was scared, but she wasn't a coward. She hadn't thought she'd live through those years in the attic, but she'd done it. She hadn't thought she'd ever find a way out of France and back to England, but she'd done it. She hadn't thought it would be possible to make a home in an idyllic village of perpetual Yuletide, but she'd done it. She hadn't thought her barricaded heart would ever fall in love, but she'd done it.

Meg had always had to come up with new plans whenever the old plan stopped working. Her fear of change might be natural, but she couldn't let it hold her back. If ever there was a man who kept his word and was the very definition of loyal, that man was Lucien le Duc. If he promised "forever," he meant bloody *forever*. The rest of the word could change anything it wished, but Lucien's heart always stayed true.

But before she could let him agree to anything… she had to tell him the full truth.

CHAPTER 16

*T*he last thing Lucien wanted was to return to his bedchamber. Rather than scurry home, he stalked back to the empty smithy instead. Here, the scorching heat from the forge would mask any pain in his heart. He could swing hammers and clang metal as loudly as necessary to drown out the relentless cacophony of his own jumbled thoughts.

Who cared if he didn't feel like working on anything? It was better than walking into his bustling cottage and confronting the happy, smiling faces of his uncle, his brother, his sister-in-law. Even the pig seemed unreasonably chipper this afternoon.

It wasn't that Lucien was at loose ends.

He'd had a plan for the past nineteen years. He still had the very same plan.

He just didn't want it anymore.

The thought of taking his rightful place in the elegant madness of French high society seemed... uninspiring. He would win back the family's lost assets—he was very much looking forward to that—but if all went well, that part of the plan would wrap up around the second of February.

Which only left the entire rest of his life to glower around ballrooms in search of someone, anyone, who remotely interested him even a fraction as much as how deeply he cared for Meg.

Huzzah. *Le plan, c'est magnifique.*

But what else was he to do? He'd asked her to marry him. She'd said no. That was that. If he was captain of his own ship, she certainly deserved to be captain of hers.

Lucien just wished it was the *same* ship.

He touched his fingers to his breast pocket, where the boat passage rested against his heart. Before, the tickets had always made him feel lighter. Now they felt incredibly heavy, as though they were leeching into his skin in order to rip new holes in his battered heart. He tossed his leather gloves aside and leaned his shoulders back against the wall.

The plan wasn't the problem. The problem was Lucien never giving anything *but* the plan a fair try.

He'd concentrated so hard on returning home to France that he never acknowledged he'd made a new home, right here in Cressmouth. The difficulty wasn't waiting to see if the villagers would ever accept him as one of their own. It was Lucien finally wielding his power to accept *them* as his own.

The world wouldn't end if he admitted he liked Cressmouth. It wouldn't even end if he admitted England itself wasn't so bad, either. Having a second home didn't mean he had to give up the first one.

He'd thought belonging to the aristocracy was what would make him important. But importance wasn't defined by a society he did not control, but rather by who Lucien decided he'd like to be important *to*.

He was already important to his family. He was even important to the village of Cressmouth. He'd *wanted* to be important to Meg, too.

Heaven knew how important she was to Lucien.

His parents had taught him to always put family first. For years, he'd defined family as his siblings and their uncle. Over the past year, he'd revised the definition to include a new brother-in-law and his two children, a new sister-in-law and her father. If Meg couldn't see that she was part of his family, too—

His breath caught in horror. Of course she couldn't *see*.

He'd told her he wanted her to marry him, but he'd skipped the part where he mentioned *why*.

The bit about joining the family? Left out entirely. The wee detail about being hopelessly, madly in love with her? Also not part of his speech. His cheeks burned. Had he thought speaking French made him more eloquent? It made him take things for granted. It highlighted his tendency to insist upon things *his* way, how *he* liked them, however *he* was more comfortable.

He should have done it in English. Garbled grammar, mortifying pronunciation, and all. It would have proven he was willing to put in effort. Willing to meet her halfway.

And he maybe should have mentioned something about love.

The sound of footsteps on gravel caused him to lift his gaze to the open door.

Meg!

Lucien leapt off his stool fast enough to send it spinning to one side. He didn't care about the stool. All he cared about was one more chance with Meg. Had she changed her mind? Was she here to say *yes* after all?

Heart beating far too fast, he hurried through the smithy to meet her.

"I'm sorry I botched the proposal." He reached for her hands.

She tucked them behind her back. "I'm not here to accept it. I—"

"Of course you shouldn't accept it. It was a terrible proposal. Mortifying, really. Which is why I—"

"We need to talk, Lucien. No one should make a decision without full knowledge of all pertinent factors, and there are a few things you—"

"I left out a lot of things. I realize that now. I'm trying to do better." He switched to English. "Marry me. I love you."

"You don't even know—"

He pulled the extra boat ticket that had been meant for his brother out of his pocket and pressed it into her hand. "Come with me.

Or not. I want you to know you have options. I want you to know that—"

"Lucien, *listen* to me." Her voice broke. "I haven't been completely honest."

His flesh went cold.

"I've never lied to you, but I left out a few important…" She rolled back her shoulders and visibly forced herself to meet his eyes. "I already have options. My mother's dowry was passed down to me. It's a plot of land."

He tilted his head in confusion. "A secret dowry is… a strange confession."

"It's land in France." Her gaze was bleak. "My mother's parents were farmers. *French* farmers. They were nobody. Not even gentry."

"I knew you weren't nobility before we even—"

"My family fought on the side of the rebellion," she blurted out. "They hated how unfair the system is. They *wanted* a revolution. People were dying out there in rural areas, and determined that if a few aristocrats had to die too in order for France to become a land of parity and equality, where a man's worth was determined by his character rather than the bloodline of long-dead ancestors—"

He took a step back. "Your family was part of the angry mobs who…"

She swallowed and gave a tight nod, her eyes tortured. "We didn't live in the same area as you, but…"

We might as well have. If we'd been neighbors then, my parents would have killed yours.

She didn't say it aloud, but Lucien heard every word anyway.

He backed away; his breath uneven, his skin cold.

"I didn't know you," she said, her voice scratchy. "And you didn't know me. But—"

"But if we had met back then, a wink and some banter would have superseded any pesky murders?" he said, his voice hollow.

"*No.*" Her face was pale. "We would never have met, not even if we lived in the same village. I would have hated you, and you would have hated me. But we didn't meet then. We met here, in Cressmouth. As equals. Without the war or the past to color our perceptions even before we could give each other a chance."

He closed his eyes and tried to block out the memories. The screams. "You have no idea what it was like."

"Neither do you." Her voice was soft, but

steel. As if she, too, had to pretend to be as unmovable as a mountain in order to prevent the past from chipping pieces of her away.

He opened his eyes. "Were your parents executed by an angry mob in the town square?"

"No." Her steady gaze did not falter. "They were stripped of their money, their home, and their dignity. Father was sent to work in a coal mine. Black dust filled his lungs, killing him slowly, a little more every day, right before our eyes. When we could see him, that was."

She visibly sucked in a breath. The next words came out slowly, painfully.

"Mother and I spent most of those years locked in an attic with other terrified women too poor to do anything but sew fancy gowns for the very rich. You might not think such a thing could kill you, but Mother was not the only one in that cramped oven of an attic who…" Her voice broke, and she lowered her gaze. "Not a town square, no. Both my parents died in my arms. One after the other."

Lucien fought through his whirlwind of emotions. Disgust, anger, betrayal, hurt.

Compassion.

He had been young the day his parents

were killed. Meg would have been even younger. She should have been tucked safely away in a schoolroom somewhere, like Lucien's brother and sister.

But she wasn't.

"You can't wait to go back to France," she said bitterly. "To reclaim your birthright. But why should wealth and privilege be your famiily's *right*, when the only thing awaiting mine was poverty and death? Is that what 'nobility' means? That an early grave should *not* happen to your parents, but *should* happen to mine?"

"No," he admitted quietly. "No one's parents should be stolen from them."

It was true. The revolution hadn't been her fight any more than it had been his. He could not blame her for what desperation had driven her family to do, any more than she could blame him for having been born in a system that... How had she put it? Defined his value based on the bloodline of his long-dead ancestors.

"My parents just wanted a chance at equality." She lifted her chin. "Which is why they fought for change. Why they fought to *matter*. Why men and women just like them did terrible things out of desperation. Out of love for their own children. Out of hope for the future and fear of death. Your parents should never have been taken from you. But nor can I blame mine for fighting for a better world for their children."

She turned to walk away.

Lucien's heart pounded.

This was why she had refused to marry him. Not because she didn't want to, not because she didn't care about him, but because she didn't believe that his love for her was more powerful than his hatred for those responsible for the terrors of the past.

"It wasn't you," he said, his voice low and scratchy.

Her startled eyes met his. "What?"

"It wasn't you," he repeated louder. "I never knew your parents, but I know *you*. If you say all they wanted was the best possible world for their children, then I believe you. You didn't know my parents, but you know *me*. When I say that all they wanted was the best possible world for their children, I hope you believe me, too."

A choking sound escaped her throat. "Of course I do. That's what any parent would want for their children. But mine—"

"—aren't here. Neither are mine." He took

her hands. "*We* are. The past may have defined us up until now, but we don't have to live in it. We have the power to shape our future. To build a new one, together. If we want to believe that love transcends the strictures of society, then let's prove it. I don't want to belong to the beau monde. I want to belong to *you*. Now and always."

She threw herself into his embrace. "I love you."

"I love you, too." He held on tight.

She felt more than perfect in his arms. She felt like home.

He whispered into her hair, "Also, not being an aristocrat doesn't make you less French."

She jerked her head back to stare at him in shock.

"I was born in *England*," she reminded him. "I'm *English*."

"Mm, with French grandparents?" He lifted a shoulder. "Someone wise once told me it's possible to be both."

The corner of her mouth twitched. "Whoever said that probably did so just to needle you."

He widened his eyes. "Is it working?"

"Splendidly."

He grinned and gestured at the project he'd been working on. "Do you want to help me roll this over to your cousin's house?"

She blinked. "It's... a miniature cart? Is it for hauling tiny calves around the dairy?"

"Close." He passed her the wooden handle. "It's for hauling a tiny niece or nephew to and from the park when we get back from France. With luck, we'll be here for the birth."

Meg's mouth fell open. "We're coming back?"

"We *have* to come back, at least for winters. At least, I do." He affected an arrogant posture. "*I* am Lucien le Duc of the Christmas dukes. Perhaps you've heard of us?"

EPILOGUE

France
The following year

They'd done it!

Meg gazed about their home with pleasure. When the lands were formally restored to the le Duc family, she and Lucien had decided to keep the previous residents on as tenants, and build a cottage on Meg's dowry land instead. It would be a few seasons before the newly planted grapes would become a profitable vineyard, but the view was incredible.

They both loved everything about their new home. It was cozy and beautiful; the perfect place to raise a family. Which was fortuitous indeed, because Meg had a suspicion...

She touched her fingertips to her belly and nestled atop a soft cushion in the bay window.

"There you are!" Lucien came swaggering out of the kitchen, cupping a silver spoon with a heap of... something. "Taste this one."

She did so, then wished she hadn't.

"It tastes *nothing* like Désirée's." Meg clutched her throat as if poisoned. "Throw it away."

He placed the spoon in her empty teacup instead and joined her in the window. "Are you spying on the neighbors?"

"We're not close enough to see through their windows." She pointed up at the sky. "I'm watching clouds instead. What does that one look like to you?"

"A redheaded champion, throbbing turgidly," he answered without hesitation.

"It does not." She snuggled into him. "It looks like a bunny. What about that one?"

He squinted. "It looks like... a swollen shaft, thick with sultry promise."

She smacked his shoulder. "Are you reading my book?"

"It's educational." He wiggled his eyebrows. "It's given me all sorts of ideas."

"Ideas on how to poison me with something that is definitely not your sister's *millefeuille*?"

"I'm getting closer," he protested, swinging her into his arms as he rose to his feet. "Do you know what else I'd like to get closer to?"

"If you say my 'milky white mounds of womanly flesh,' so help me God..." she warned him.

He opened his eyes wide in faux innocence.

"It's like you can read my mind," he whispered, as he carried her to their bedroom. "Except I was going to add something about the pert rosebuds protruding from them with innocent desire."

"My nipples are brown," she reminded him. "They don't look anything like roses."

"They're sort of a tea-with-milk color," he conceded. "I'm working on an appropriately flowery metaphor."

She gasped in horror. "Are you *writing* a book?"

"I'm in the research stage," he informed her. He tossed her into the center of the bed and pounced atop her. "Want to help me with my investigations?"

"Only for the rest of my life." She wrapped her arms about him and pulled him close.

THE END

What madcap romantic entanglements will occur at the Duke of Nottingvale's long-awaited Christmastide house party?

Join the fun in *Dawn with a Duke*, the next romance in the *12 Dukes of Christmas* series!

ACKNOWLEDGMENTS

As always, I could not have written this book without the invaluable support of my critique partner, beta readers, and editors. Huge thanks go out to Erica Monroe and Tessa Shapcott. You are the best!

Lastly, I want to thank the *12 Dukes of Christmas* facebook group, my *Historical Romance Book Club,* and my fabulous street team. Your enthusiasm makes the romance happen.

Thank you so much!

THANK YOU FOR READING

Love talking books with fellow readers?

Join the *Historical Romance Book Club* for prizes, books, and live chats with your favorite romance authors:
Facebook.com/
groups/HistRomBookClub

Check out the *12 Dukes of Christmas* facebook group for giveaways and exclusive content:
Facebook.com/groups/DukesOf-
Christmas

Join the *Rogues to Riches* facebook group for insider info and first looks at future books in the series:

Facebook.com/groups/RoguesToRiches

Check out the *Dukes of War* facebook group for giveaways and exclusive content:

Facebook.com/groups/DukesOfWar

And check out the official website for sneak peeks and more:

www.EricaRidley.com/books

ABOUT THE AUTHOR

Erica Ridley is a *New York Times* and *USA Today* best-selling author of historical romance novels.

In the new *12 Dukes of Christmas* series, enjoy witty, heartwarming Regency romps nestled in a picturesque snow-covered village. After all, nothing heats up a winter night quite like finding oneself in the arms of a duke!

Her two most popular series, the *Dukes of War* and *Rogues to Riches*, feature roguish peers and dashing war heroes who find love amongst the splendor and madness of Regency England.

When not reading or writing romances, Erica can be found riding camels in Africa, zip-lining through rainforests in Central America, or getting hopelessly lost in the middle of Budapest.

～

Let's be friends! Find Erica on:
www.EricaRidley.com

CPSIA information can be obtained
at www.ICGtesting.com
Printed in the USA
BVHW030154310320
576447BV00001B/133

9 781943 794676